VIETNAM

BOOK ONE

I PLEDGE ALLEGIANCE

CHRIS LYNCH

★

SCHOLASTIC INC.

This book was originally published in hardcover by Scholastic Press in 2011.

ISBN 978-0-545-27030-4

12 11 10 9 8 7 6 5 4 3 2 1   12 13 14 15 16 17/0

Printed in the U.S.A. 40
First paperback printing, October 2012

The text type was set in Sabon MT.
Book design by Christopher Stengel

PART
ONE

The Nightmare

If friendship has an opposite, it has to be war.

Do you know what it feels like to watch your best friend die right in front of you? To watch the skin roll back off his skull like the pages of a book thrown into a fire? I do. Do you know what it feels like to watch your three oldest best friends die just like that, right in front of your eyes, and to know you are responsible, that you could have done something about it but didn't?

I know exactly what that feels like.

I am the last one to The Curb. That's the curb in front of Janelle's Market, diagonally across from the high school. Ivan, Rudi, Beck, and I have met here nearly every school morning for the last four years. The whole high school game is just about done, one week to go, but there's no need to break up old routines just yet.

So I mention last night's dream.

"Oh, no, Morris," Ivan protests. "No, no, not the dream again. Please . . ."

I've had the dream a lot. It's a nightmare. Ivan shouldn't be surprised to hear I've had it again. I watch the news. These days, even if you don't watch the news, you watch the news. It finds you. It's everywhere. The whole world is Vietnam now. The surprise is that everybody in the entire United States is not having the same nightmare as me, every single night.

"Well, yeah, Ivan, I had the dream again."

"Well, yeah, Morris, we have heard it all before so we don't need to hear it again."

There's a pause. It's not suspense, really, because it always goes pretty much the same after I've had the dream.

"I could hear it again," says Rudi, right on cue. He looks so serious and plumped up with anticipation, I almost don't want to retell it now. Because it ain't gonna end any different.

"Does telling it again really help anybody?" Beck asks. He is sitting beside Rudi and gesturing toward him with his eyes, so we all know who he means by *anybody*.

I shrug. "I don't know. Maybe."

"Ah, jeez," Ivan butts in angrily. "*I'll* tell it."

I stare at him like he's nuts. "You're going to tell *my* dream?"

"Why not? I've heard it a thousand times. I can tell it. And a lot better than you."

"Fine, Ivan — go ahead, tell my dream."

"Right. The dream starts with a wicked firefight. I get shot a lot of times, but I don't even burp. I'm killing guys all over the place. Beck is filling out the newspaper crossword from behind a small hill —"

"I don't remember that part," Beck interrupts.

"Hey," Ivan says, and he seems to be taking himself seriously here, "was it *your* dream, Beck?"

"No," I cut back in, "it was *mine*, so —"

"Right," Ivan goes on, "and Morris is crying and trying to dig his way home through the ground with his fingernails, but his nails are already bitten down so much —"

"I was never crying," I say. "Not until very late, anyway, near the end of the whole dream, almost."

"Can everyone just please let Ivan tell the dream the right way, please?" Rudi asks. Begs, really. Poor Rudi. He needs this.

"Just get it over with," says Beck. His mind is always working at about twice the speed as the rest of our minds, so it's like he's already been to the end of the conversation and back and is impatient for the rest of us to catch up.

"Right. So this guy's bawlin', this one's trying to figure out a seven-letter word for *MommyPleaseCome-GetMeNow,* and I'm collecting Vietcong kills like they're baseball cards."

"Yeah?" Rudi says, his voice rising up there in I Believe It Land. Rudi thinks every story is a real story.

"Oh, yeah," Ivan says, looking up at the sky, half believing it himself.

"What about me?" Rudi asks anxiously. "Me?"

Ivan's still admiring his bravery and cunning on that cinema screen he's seeing in the sky. He likes what he sees, smiles at what he sees. Then he looks down into Rudi's waiting face with its giant trusting eyes and puffy mouth pulled tight with nerves.

Even Ivan can't do it. Even Ivan, who has never been much for feelings — his or anybody else's — can't let Rudi get in the line of fire. No dream heroics for Rudi.

"You aren't there, Rude," Ivan says. "You're back at the base, cooking Swedish meatballs over flat noodles for us to have when we get back. Nobody's shootin' at you, and you're not shootin' at anybody else."

"No-shootie Rudi," Beck chips in.

Now there is very obvious pleasure on Rudi's face.

"I could definitely do that," Rudi says. "Swedish meatballs, man — I love Swedish meatballs." Then he turns to me, snappy. "How come you never tell the story like that, Morris?"

All three of them stare at me now. Rudi's big trusting eyes dominate.

"Because it's a lie, Rudi, man," I say sadly, rightly. "It's a lie."

It's a lie.

Because my dream is a crystal-clear vision of torn flesh and burned flesh and the end of everything we know, all dying there in the scorching jungle of Vietnam. Four great friends, one mighty beast of a friendship, shredded to bits. It's my dream, and I've had it pretty much the same way at least fifty times. I'm the guy who wakes up sweating as if my actual body has taken me to that jungle while I slept. So maybe my body already knows.

All four of us die every single time. Sometimes it's in a different order. Sometimes we all die at once. Sometimes it's a wall of fire and sometimes a hail of bullets. Sometimes a stabbing, sometimes an explosion. Or a drowning.

But always we die, every time.

And it's my fault, every time.

Because I let it happen. Which is why I can't let it happen.

Which is why we have the pledge.

CHAPTER TWO

I Pledge Allegiance

We have a pact for everything. I suppose it was me who got it started.

We all go along, once a pact makes sense. And a pact makes sense every time something bigger than us comes along and looks like enough of a threat that we need to band together. It's our response to every scary or confusing or just plain overwhelming force that seems capable of destroying the four-man fortress that we've built.

Evelyn DelValle was such a force.

We were in sixth grade. We were eleven-going-on-twelve, except for Rudi, who was twelve-going-on-thirteen-going-on-seven. Evelyn was always there in the same school with us, from first grade. She was a good kid, as girls go, not a close friend to any of us, but not a whole load of trouble, either. As girls go.

Then, suddenly, she was a whole load of trouble.

"I can't stop thinking about her," Beck said, staring like a dolt across the school yard. Our class was playing foot hockey with a sponge ball, and Beck was our goalie. He had just let something like his eighth goal roll by, between the two balled-up coats that were the goalposts. One of the coats was mine, and it was just before Christmas break. I was cold.

"Well, you *better* stop thinking about her," Ivan said, walking right up and giving Beck a flat smack to the forehead with the heel of his hand.

Beck appeared like he didn't even notice.

"Beck, man," I said, "I didn't give up my warm coat for this. Get your head in the game." Normally, he was an unbeatable goalie. And worst of all was that we were playing against the seventh graders. Even though they were older and mostly bigger, we were as good as them. We just were. Sometimes you get a group of guys who just work together, blend together, and they defy the odds, and this class was a class of those guys. The sevenths hated us for it, the way it upended the whole nature of things. And their relationship with the eighths was the normal seventh-eighth relationship, meaning they got spanked by the older guys regularly. Yesterday, as a matter of fact.

Which wasn't good for us. One of the penalties for losing was a mass wedgie, which the losers had to administer to *each other*, while the winners supervised, hooted, and applauded.

The stakes were high.

"What's wrong with him?" Rudi asked, joining our goal-crease conference.

"Nothing wrong with me," Beck said, a stupid happy glaze all over his face.

"Yes, there is," Ivan said, gesturing toward Rudi. "You look like *him*."

"Yeah," Rudi said accusingly. "What's that all about?"

"Right," I said, turning and looking in the direction of Beck's faraway gaze. There was a small gathering of girls doing a whole lot of very distracting nothing against one of the far school walls. "I'll be back."

I ran in the direction of Evelyn DelValle and company. I didn't get twenty yards before I heard the familiar noise of us giving up another goal behind me.

"Hey," I said to Evelyn — not too harshly, but not quite friendly, either. "You gotta cut it out."

I could see her in profile as I approached, and I was certain she could see me. She had uncommonly large brown eyes that I hadn't noticed so much before . . . but at this moment I was sure would give her amazing peripheral vision.

"What?" she said, turning sort of slow motion my way. "I need to cut something out? What am I doing?"

She was doing it again.

Well, this was embarrassing. I came over to lodge a complaint and to tell her to cut it out, and I couldn't even put into words what she had to cut out.

But she knew she was doing it.

Her eyes were so big. So amazing.

"How come you never talked to me before?" she said, touching the back of my hand with her index finger. I felt it in my knees.

Suddenly, speech was a foreign and painful process. Every word came up like I was coughing out a peach pit.

"Oh, I talked. Before. I talked to you."

"Not really. You never talked to me for real. And now, for the first time, you do, and it's all unfriendly and telling me to cut it out."

"I'm sorry," I said like a simp.

"That's okay," she said. "Now we're talking, so it will be easier from now on. We can talk."

"We can?" By now I had no recollection of why I had come over here. But I was really, really, really glad I had.

Until I got wedgied. Lifted right up off my feet, in plain view of Evelyn DelValle and everything.

"Ahhh-ahhh," I screamed, quite high pitched. This wasn't going very well at all.

Everybody was laughing — my guys, the seventh grade guys. Apparently, we had taken a beating of biblical proportions while I was busy trying to rescue our goaltender from Evelyn. Also apparently, my efforts came to nothing anyway since, while I was busy drifting into the powerful gravitational grip of this girl, poor sap Beck stood there stupid like before. He didn't tend goal, he didn't speak or move. He just stared.

We were in love, both me and Beck, and we knew it — which made the simultaneous wedgies even harder to take, what with the lady herself witnessing, and laughing robustly at, our humiliation.

So what was going to happen, with two of the four of us mental over the one girl?

"Wow," said Rudi, loud and naked and stupid. He just looked at Evelyn and said "wow" again.

She was wow. All of a sudden, she was wow and wower and wowest, but you didn't have to blurt it right out loud.

Which is why Ivan stepped up, practically bowed to the princess, then body-slammed Rudi right there on the pavement.

To the untrained eye, that was random violence.

But to us, it was a lot more. That was Ivan going wobbly over a girl.

So the team was complete. Four for four.

"Now what?" said Beck as the four of us walked

home together that afternoon. It usually was down to Beck to be the guy rationalizing things out. Even if he did still have that bashed-in-the-head-with-a-ball-peen-hammer-or-possibly-it's-love look on his face.

"Now what, what?" I asked.

"You know what, Morris. The Evelyn situation. Jeez, everybody in the whole school yard could see it. You really embarrassed yourself out there."

"*I* embarrassed myself?"

"Yeah, Beck, what are you talking about?" Ivan jumped in. "If anybody was embarrassing, it was Mister WOW here. Smooth move there, Rudi."

Rudi started getting flustered, his voice rising into that whistle-tone that signals his discombobulation.

"You dumped me on my head! On my *head*. If anybody was really being embarrassing, it was you."

"Me?" Ivan laughed the triumphant laugh of disgust. "Rudi, I have dumped you on your head about a thousand times. And they were all for just cause, and you know it. You even liked it most of the time. So I can't see your point about why this time was such a big . . ."

It was becoming apparent that nobody was going to be able to see anybody's point anytime soon.

"So," Beck spoke up, coming to the same conclusion, "like I said, what now?"

"Will somebody please tell me what we're talking about?" asked Rudi.

"I suppose that's up to Evelyn," I said.

"No," Ivan said, his serious voice coming on, the deep, slow, serious voice. "No, it's not up to Evelyn."

"What are you, a caveman?" I asked him. "You gonna *tell* her that she has to like you and that's that?"

"Maybe she doesn't like any of us," Rudi said.

"Maybe," Ivan said, "it doesn't matter. Because if she did like one of us, we would have a problem, wouldn't we?"

There was a silence for several seconds as we all tried to muscle up the strength to tell a decent lie.

But of course a lie wouldn't help. We all knew we'd have a problem.

"What's more important, right?" asked Beck.

"What's more important than what?" asked Rudi. "I hate it when it gets like this. I don't follow anything."

Ivan stopped walking, turned around, and let Rudi walk right into him.

"Sorry," Rudi said, like it was his fault.

Ivan grinned real hard, grabbed Rudi's big dopey head in his hands, and squeezed. Then he shook it all around.

"Than us, Rudi, man? What is more important than

us? Than *this*?" Ivan gestured all around — at me, at Beck, at himself, using Rudi's head as a pointer. Rudi looked scared at first, then very, very happy.

"Nothing," said Rudi. "Nothing is more important than us, man."

Ivan let him go, turned, and started walking again.

"That's right. Nothing is more important to us than us. So if anything is going to come between us . . ."

"That thing is off-limits," I said.

We were crossing the big intersection just before the point where we splintered into our four directions.

"Evelyn DelValle," Ivan said with a big gap in the middle there, "is off-limits."

There was a rusty squeak of sadness behind me.

"But I love Evelyn DelValle," said Rudi.

I slapped his back gently. "You can keep loving her," I told him.

"But keep it to yourself," Ivan said.

I put the stamp on it. "It's a pledge, then."

The other guys all moaned loudly as we got to the corner. "Gee, does everything have to be a *pledge*?" Beck grumped. "It's not a pledge."

"It's not a pledge," Ivan said. "It's a *thing*, not a pledge."

"It's a pledge," I said, "and you all know it."

We split off right there, our four ways to the four winds, and we knew we had pledged.

Even if they all kept moaning and groaning until I was in my front door, practically.

It was a pledge.

CHAPTER THREE

When You Need 'Em Most

We had a pledge for just about everything.

When Ivan was grounded for punching somebody who everybody agreed needed punching, and it happened just when *The Good, the Bad and the Ugly* came out, we all agreed we wouldn't see the movie until the four of us could see it together. It meant blocking our ears for another two weeks while every other thrilled and excited cowboy in town couldn't shut up about it.

By the time we saw it, at the Rialto in Roslindale Square, I know it was a better movie than the one everybody else saw.

When we made the jump from everybody-plays Little League baseball to the more competitive Babe Ruth League and not one team drafted Rudi, the other three of us pledged to take the year off. That was the most boring summer of my life, and the point where I realized I loved baseball even more than I did Evelyn DelValle, but we got through it.

When Rudi first joined us, it was the first day of fourth grade. Except for Rudi. For him it was the *second* first day of fourth grade, since he had done the whole year already and was back for more.

That first day, we did what everybody did to a kid who got kept back. We teased and tormented him like the helpless, harmless hamster that he was. I didn't even think anything of it. Matter of fact, I didn't even think that *he* thought anything of it. I simply believed, in my lead box of a young boy's head, that this was the way guys did stuff and everybody was more or less understanding of that situation.

Until I found Rudi, on the way home, on his knees. I was walking on my own up Centre Street when I passed the turn splitting off into Moraine Street and South Huntington Avenue. And there were two of Rudi's former classmates, big-shot fifth graders now, dumping the contents of Rudi's book bag into the gutter, laughing. Rudi was in praying position, just off the curb.

"You ain't doin' it right," one of the kids said.

"Of course he's not doin' it right. Rudi never did nothin' right, which is why he's in fourth grade forever. Right, Rudi-doody?"

"That's right," said Rudi, hands folded, voice cracking.

Right? *Right?* Okay, maybe this wasn't way different

from the stuff we were doing to him in the school yard, but . . . it wasn't right.

You know what else wasn't right? When the two guys looked at me, I walked on.

I left Rudi right there, on his knees, in the gutter, with all his books and pencils and papers splashed around him.

I dreamed about it that night. I still dream it sometimes now.

I didn't bother Rudi the next day, though it was still a popular sport. I just couldn't do it. Don't get me wrong: This was not because I was a good guy all of a sudden and nobody else was. It was because I felt like a bad guy, and nobody else seemed to. I watched. I didn't do anything to interfere with other people bothering Rudi, so I couldn't have been all that good. But I also watched everybody else, and I could see that they didn't see anything wrong with what they were doing. It was natural, it was the way of things, and they were all right.

For some reason, though, I had an impulse. To invite friends home with me for the afternoon.

So we walked together, me and Beck and Ivan, toward my house, the regular route.

"What are we going to do?" Beck asked.

"I don't know," I said. "Stuff. The usual stuff."

"The usual stuff at your house is kind of boring, no offense," said Ivan.

"No offense, no problem," I said. "I'll work on it. It'll be less boring."

Then we came up to Moraine Street. And there he was.

Rudi, on his knees in the street, among all his things. Praying, just like yesterday.

For several seconds we all just stood there, staring, taking in the scene. Actually, I was watching my friends while they took in the scene. As if I needed their reactions to tell me what I should think.

I didn't have to wait long.

"Oh, no," Beck said. "*No.*"

"Uh-uh," Ivan said, stomping toward the scene.

Now I knew how to feel: outraged.

"Hey," Ivan said to the guys, the pair of big fifth graders named Arthur and Teddy we knew too well from hockey battles, and I knew too well from the day before.

The two turned quickly and nervously. Then they changed right away to defiant, like you do when you know you're guilty. "Hey *what*?" snapped Arthur.

"Hey, leave the kid alone," said Ivan.

"What's it to you?" asked Teddy.

"He's a friend of ours," said Beck.

Rudi, still on his knees, allowed himself a small smile.

"Don't get too excited," Ivan said to Rudi.

"Don't lie. He's nobody's friend. Get lost and mind your own business."

I walked over to Rudi and pulled him up by the arm, since he didn't seem capable of getting up on his own.

"He's our business," said Beck firmly.

So we were all standing there with the tension building. The big fifth graders looked tough up to a point. But there was enough school-yard history here — especially with Ivan — to know it wasn't as simple as: older guys win. And their faces showed it.

"Oh," Teddy tried, "so it's gonna be four on two, is it?"

"Don't be a jerk," Ivan said. "This guy" — pointing his thumb at Rudi — "obviously doesn't count. And this guy" — me — "couldn't fight his way out of a wet paper bag."

Here was my chance to come up big. "Ah, I think I probably could," I said.

The point was made, anyway. Ivan and Beck stepped right up close to the big guys, and stood there and stood there.

You could smell in the air how this was going. Ivan alone was enough of a force to settle this. We were all just waiting now to see how it was going to fizzle out.

"Rudi, pick up your stuff," Beck said, staring down Teddy the whole time.

Rudi practically dove to the ground to collect his books and what all. The jerks took that as the break they needed. They walked, first backward, then turning away up Moraine Street. Arthur made an embarrassing little attempt at waving us off dismissively, but Ivan wouldn't even let him get away with that much.

"Try this again, boys," he called out, "and you'll be picking his stuff off the street next time. With your lips."

We watched them slither away, and it felt like a long time. Moraine Street is long, sloping down slightly to the pond, and by the time they crested it, they had checked back over their shoulders three times, slouching a little more each time they saw us again.

That was a whippin'.

That was our pal Ivan.

"Thanks," Rudi gushed, rushing up and shaking Ivan's hand crazily.

Ivan sneered at him, then took his book bag and dumped everything out again on the ground.

That, too, was our pal Ivan.

But Rudi was a lot happier picking his stuff up that time.

And that was a moment, *the* moment. Something

changed there for us as a foursome. Maybe it was kicked in by Rudi being needy and making us feel needed. It was as if we had adopted an orphan and we could never give him back. As if the responsibility changed us somehow. I don't know for sure. What I do know for sure is that from then on we hung together, fought together, thought together, fought each other, from then on, forever. Something clicked there, that made us *more* than before, more than four.

It made us, if it's okay to say this, *better*.

CHAPTER FOUR

No, I Won't Be Afraid, No, I Won't Be Afraid

When Ivan had his first punch-up with his old man, he stayed at my house for four days. When Rudi's mother developed a habit of forgetting to pack him a lunch, Beck's mom developed a habit of packing an extra sandwich and a second bag of Fritos into his.

When my dad died, all three of the guys slept on my bedroom floor every night until I told them they could leave. Then they stayed until I told them they *had* to leave.

We all chose the same high school when the time came. Even though Beck could have chosen some special genius school, he decided not to. Even though Rudi could have flunked out at any moment, he managed not to.

And when the Vietnam War started pouring into my living room, just like everybody else's living room, and I started getting nightmares, we all pledged none of us was going to go over there voluntarily. I just couldn't live with it.

Thursday night, Arboretum. Ivan and Rudi bring the drinks, I bring a bucket of Fontaine's amazing boneless fried chicken, Beck brings a pan of his own butterscotch brownies made from scratch, because Beck is a freak. We meet at the top of Peters Hill to look out over treetops at the skyline and talk ragtime about the bigness of our futures and the smallness of Boston in comparison.

I'm doing all that by myself for a while, as I'm the first one there. This chicken is amazing, and without the bones it is so easy to buzz through it. If they don't arrive soon, I cannot be held responsible.

I do like the skyline. I do like the city. It's not too small at all, really, and I believe I could be happy here for a long time to come. I'll still talk ragtime, though.

"Hey," Beck says, tromping up behind me. "Want a brownie? They're still warm."

I can smell them. I don't even turn around.

"Can't have brownies yet. We're still on savory." I wave a piece of chicken in the air. Like a fish jumping to a fly, he comes alongside and snaps it out of my hand. He sits down next to me on the block of granite that serves as our bench, facing out at the city and the world on the far side of the city. "And the drinks are nowhere to be seen yet. Can't do brownies without something to wash them down."

"Could try," he says.

"See, Beck, man, that's where you start to worry me. That's where your whole *scientist* thing starts to look like *mad* scientist."

"You think?"

"I do. I know you are smarter than everybody everywhere, but sometimes that can get in the way. That's why you need me, so my normal level of intelligence can keep you in touch with the rest of us."

He is examining the piece of chicken he has just bitten into. He is admiring it. "Thanks, Morris," he says. "We'll never discuss it again."

"Well, good. What are you ever going to do without me at college, Beck?"

"I'll just embarrass myself, Morris," he says, putting a light headlock on me as we still stare in the same direction over Boston. I can hear inside his head as he chews.

The truth is, his brownies are kind of dry. But I refuse to be the first person to tell him he's failed at something.

"Hey, is this what happens when I show up late?" Ivan asks.

We turn to see him swaggering toward us, an open can of Moxie in one hand and four more hanging off the rings in his other.

"Ugh," I say, "again with the Moxie? That stuff tastes like carbonated tires."

"Quiet. Nobody needs Moxie more than you do."

"You were supposed to bring a full six," Beck says, pulling a can off the ring.

"Yeah, well," Ivan says as I pluck another of the cans, "I mugged myself on the way over. I put up a brave fight, though. Where's Bozo, anyway?"

"Not here yet," I say, and offer Ivan the chicken bucket. He reaches in and grabs a fistful of flesh, like he's getting bait to go fishing.

"Well, he better get here soon."

"Aw, you miss him," Beck says.

"Quiet, Brownie, I'm only thinking of you two." He takes a seat on a boulder a few feet away and swallows a chunk of chicken whole, like a snake would with a frog.

"Us?" Beck asks.

"Yeah," Ivan says, holding up the ring with two last cans dangling. "If Rudi doesn't show up, what are you two gonna drink?"

Fortunately, we don't have to answer that, because Rudi comes walking up the face of the steep hill in front of us. It is not the normal way we come up, but the normal way of anything is always optional for Rudi. We watch him for a while, in the bluey evening light, and it seems to take him forever to reach us. It is a tough hill, but not this tough.

"What's that he's carrying?" Beck asks.

It's white. It's paper. It flaps in his hand in the light breeze, catching the remaining light as if it is some kind of signal flag he's waving in surrender.

Finally, he reaches the top of the hill, stands there silently in front of us. Kind of a cool picture, I think for a few seconds — Rudi standing tall with the skyline and the first stars hanging there behind him.

But only for a few seconds. It becomes obvious pretty quickly that this is not cool at all.

He holds the paper out in Beck's direction — shoves it at him, really.

"Does this mean what I think it means?" Rudi's voice is crying. He's not crying, is what he'd say, but his voice surely is. "Tell me what it means, Beck, man. You're smart, I'm stupid. Tell me I got it wrong, and it doesn't mean what I think."

It's Beck's assignment, but I read over his shoulder.

**You are hereby directed to present yourself
for Armed Forces Physical Examination...**

It feels like it takes an hour for Beck and me to sit there reading this one page. Rudi doesn't make a move, becoming just another dark lump of granite standing here on the hilltop. The silence is broken by Ivan pulling the tab off the top of another can. He has three of them now, decorating his fingers like sharp, curly silver rings. "So?" he says.

Beck looks up to Rudi. "Have a brownie, pal."

Now Rudi starts crying for real. But he does take a brownie, then wedges himself tight on the rock chair between Beck and me.

We had a pledge for this. Of course. We hardly ever talked about it, because, I think, nobody wanted to consider this possibility. At least that's why I didn't talk about it. It did not bear thinking about.

Rudi is nineteen, a year older than the rest of us — because of getting kept back in fourth grade. We tended to forget. But the government failed to forget. So Rudi was eligible for the draft once he graduated and didn't go for any kind of deferral.

The three of us sit there, reading and rereading words on a page, trying to rearrange them into something better.

"What?" Ivan asks.

"Why would they want me?" Rudi asks earnestly.

" 'Cause you are a good man, man," Beck tells him.

When we first and last discussed this, we all agreed that if one of us got drafted, we were all drafted. We knew we wouldn't be together, physically. But we also felt that we would be together. *In it. Together.* The only way it should be and could be. Ivan's opinion was that we would have to go just to balance the Rudi effect, because he was capable of getting shot to pieces *and* losing the war all by himself.

The three of us are still staring at the page when, *whap*, it snaps out of the air and we see Ivan standing over us, reading for himself.

He reads. Reads further. One foot starts tapping, like there is music only he can hear, and it is coming up in notes off that very page. Then his hips start swinging, his shoulders start shimmying.

He is doing this little dance as he lowers the page and we are exposed to this broad, demented, delirious grin. He turns his back to us, continues his little silent shimmy-dance a few feet into the direction of the city skyline. He holds the page in the air, and he lets out a roar.

"We . . . are . . . goin' . . . to . . . *Nam*, boys!"

I can hear his big-barrel voice roll down the grassy slope of Peters Hill, through the trees, through the neighborhoods, out of Roslindale, through JP, past Fenway and Brookline and out into downtown, bounce off of everyplace we have ever known and up into the air to sweep back to us again on our little spot on our old hill.

Ivan does a touchdown celebration, spikes the letter into the dirt, and comes rushing over to shake the hand of poor, blindsided Rudi.

"Congratulations, boy, and thank you, and I am sorry, but, *wooo-hooo!*"

Rudi, on his feet and as confused as he will ever be, is shaking hands wildly in response, and crying, and smiling. Because Rudi idolizes Ivan.

Even Ivan can see the six different kinds of expression warring across Rudi's face. He grabs him now by the shoulders.

"Rudi, buddy, you're gonna be fine. You're gonna be more than fine. You're gonna be a man. And you're gonna be a hero."

"Or maybe he'll fail his physical," I say hopefully.

"This boy ain't failing nothin'," Ivan says, squeezing Rudi's shoulders harder.

"Will I?" Rudi asks. "Ivan, will I be a hero?"

"Absolutely."

"But . . . I peed myself. When I opened it. I peed myself."

"Jeez, Rudi," Beck says, hopping up off the rock. "You didn't even change your pants."

Rudi is, in fact, very damp.

"I came running," Rudi says. "I had to. Had to see you guys . . ."

Ivan breaks off into a one-man conga line. "The Rudi peed his pants *dance/* The Rudi peed his pants . . ."

"Do you *have* to be this happy?" I ask him.

"You know I do."

I do know. He was never a fan of this particular pledge, and it is to his credit that he went along with it despite everything. To be honest, it was never a very Ivan pledge to begin with.

"Army, baby. The armored cavalry, just like my old man. My dad spent World War Two riding tanks and slapping crybabies all over North Africa and Europe with General Patton. They were pals, you know. Did you know that?"

We know that. He knows we know that. He loves telling us anyway.

"Wait 'til I tell my dad," he says. "He always thought Morris's pledge was an ol' nancy pledge anyway — no offense, Morris."

"Of course not," I say, afraid he might start the slapping any minute.

"Now we got a real pledge, boys," he says. "A *man's* pledge."

Instead, he picks up the letter, smoothes it out against his leg.

On this point, I can't disagree with him. We've been together, through whatever, since forever. And when we pledged that none of us was going to Vietnam without all of us going to Vietnam . . . well, if we didn't mean that, then we are meaningless, aren't we?

Ivan walks up to Rudi, hands him back his letter. He stands back and shoots him a crisp and serious right-angle salute that he learned from his father and his father's father and his father's father's father.

Rudi, still a watery mess, does his best version of a salute in return.

Then, for the first time and, I can assure you, for the last time, the four of us step up into a four-man hug. We hold it for a good minute while I look over Beck's shoulder at the skyline of Boston already looking very, very far away.

CHAPTER FIVE

One Tree, Four Branches

There was never any doubt where Ivan was going. He didn't even sleep that night, waiting up 'til the recruiting office opened. When he said Army, he meant Army.

Beck had the hardest time. See, Beck is meant for better things. He's a brilliant guy, from a family of smarts. His house is a strange place, always filled with music, with paintings all over the walls, and all of that stuff is created by the people who actually live there. His dad works with computers. Who works with computers? Who works with computers, paints, and makes music? I mean, I am mostly not a dummy, but to me those things come down from *elsewhere*, you know? They are not produced by people, much less by people you ask to pass the gravy.

But these are Beck's people, and Beck's people are not happy. The boy has a scholarship to study physics at the University of Wisconsin–Madison, and that's what his people want to see him doing. The draft won't even bother him for at least four more years, not even counting graduate school. And graduate school to his family is like primary school for most of us: You bring shame on the whole clan by failing to complete it.

Beck has nothing to gain by signing up. He is, by far, making the greatest sacrifice with this pledge.

"You don't have to go," I tell him.

"Yes, I do."

We are back at Peters Hill, walking up through the few pre–Revolutionary War headstones that slant along the street side, with their skulls and crossbones and childlike death carvings. Beck stops, staring at them, and we don't bother going to the top. It's a perfect June day, sunny, cool in the shade, just-hot in the sun. We sit, back-to-back, with the thin slab of a former somebody named Weld between us, propping us up after just sitting there doing nothing for two hundred years.

"I wouldn't go if I were you," I say.

"You're lying," he says. "And if you weren't lying, Ivan would shoot you if you tried not to go."

I think about it, staring directly into the sun even though I know how bad that is for me. Trying to blind myself before induction, maybe. I am that scared.

"Too true," I say. "He wouldn't shoot you, though. You know it. Nobody would shoot you, and nobody would think anything bad about you if you just went to Madison. You're worth more than this, Beck, man."

I can feel, just slightly, Mr. Weld's stone moving my way, pressing on me.

"Is this guy trying to get up," I ask, "or are you actually pushing his grave marker over?"

I look over my shoulder when he doesn't respond. I don't even think he's aware of pushing.

"We all have to go, Morris," he says. "I've already had to go to war with my parents and my sisters and my uncles — if I have to fight you over it, too, I'm going to have nothing left for the Vietcong."

Vietcong. Even their name has come to scare me.

"Still . . ."

"Still, we made a pledge, and it was a great pledge. I'm going. I just about managed to convince my dad that being in the Air Force counts as continuing my aeronautical education, and with Wisconsin deferring my admission until I get back, everything's fine."

Everything's fine. Everything's fine. He watches TV just like I do, and he knows how fine everything is not.

"Fine," I say.

"Fine," he says.

Rudi passes his physical. Nobody doubted that he would, since Rudi's shortcomings tend not to be below the neck. In a way, you could say he failed by passing his physical, which is all very Rudi.

"What are they going to expect me to do, Morris? Are they going to give me, you know, a job or something?"

"I would expect that's what they will do. But whatever job they give you, remember your real job is just to be careful and come home safe."

"I hear ya. I just don't know if I'll know how to do that. I'm gonna get killed, Morris. I don't have a chance, and you know it, and everybody else knows it."

If you were going purely on things like common sense and reason, then he would be right. Rudi is going to die in Vietnam just as sure as the Red Sox are going to fail to win the World Series. That's just the way the universe is set up.

"No, I don't know that," I say to him. We have just left the Navy recruiting office, which we had agreed to visit as soon as he got his physical results and his notice to report. I signed up without even listening to the guy's pitch about the joys of life on the high and low seas.

"I'm gonna die, Morris. I mess up most things, and even the things I do the best at, I don't do very well. Even I know that when you don't do the Marines very well while you are in Vietnam, you don't just get kept back. You get bloody and dead."

"Why are we here, Rudi?" Here, at the moment, is a booth in the front window of Brigham's Ice Cream on Boylston Street downtown.

"We're here because I was crying — again — and because I am such a baby, you had to promise me an ice cream."

"We are here because I joined the Navy. And why did I join the Navy?"

"Because the Navy watches over the Marines, and you wanted to be able to watch over me."

He's learned his lines well. That's the story I told him.

That's the story I told myself.

"Correct, my friend. I am gonna be there with you. And so is Ivan. And Beck. As long as we're all there, then we're together, like always. And as long as we're together, nothing's going to happen to you, or to any of us. Okay?"

The sundaes arrive. His is chocolate with marshmallow, nuts, and multicolored jimmies. Mine is butterscotch with whipped cream and chocolate jimmies. The sun is shining through the window, and the street outside is happy busy. What could be wrong?

"Okay, Morris, man, if you say so."

"I do say so. Now eat your sundae."

"Fine," he says, digging in and almost smiling. "But tell me again now, who are we fighting, and how come?"

I really wish he would stop asking me this.

"We are fighting alongside the South Vietnamese against the North Vietnamese. The North has gotten aggressive against the South."

"Like the Civil War here."

"Well . . ."

"But we were on the North side then, and the South side now."

"That part is kind of irrelevant."

"Why are we mixed up in it if those two are fighting? I mean, it's sad, but it's also far away, so why should we care?"

"Your ice cream is melting, Rudi."

"I like it a little melty."

"It's about Communism versus Democracy. Remember all that stuff from school? And from the four times I already tried to explain it to you?"

"I remember it, Morris. It's just that, sorry, but you've never explained it in a way that makes sense."

There is a good reason for that. I wish I understood it better myself.

"*Ours is not to question why*, pal."

"Now *that* quote I remember. It ends with *die*, right?"

"You're right — I *am* doing a lousy job of making this make sense. Maybe you should stop expecting me to make sense of things, Rudi."

"I'll never expect you to stop making sense."

He has finished his ice cream and reaches over to take mine. It's okay. This is the way it always winds up.

"How in the world did they ever pick me, Morris? If they didn't draft me . . ."

"That's why they call it the Selective Service, man. You meet some qualifications, then after that, they're just plucking your name out of a barrel."

"Well, the service can't be very selective if they want me, that's all I'll say."

I stand up, even though he has several spoonfuls left. It's his signal to shovel. He gets to it, and I take a scan all around me, looking at bright and shiny Brigham's, here just the way it always has been, the way I figure it always will be. The checkerboard tiles, the ceiling fans, the long counter with the spinning seats.

It will be here when I get back. Of course it will. Everything will.

"*Arrrr,*" Rudi says, getting up, wincing, grabbing his forehead. Like always.

"Froze your brain, right?"

He nods, his hand nodding right along with his head.

"Stay just like that, my man, and you will be fine." I grab him in a headlock and haul him out into the bright sunshine and business of Boylston Street. "Don't let anybody thaw out that brain of yours."

"Who would want to?" he asks.

"I'm guessing the Marine Corps might want to take a shot at it."

"A shot?" He seems slightly alarmed.

"I don't think they will go quite as far as shooting you. But they will put a lot of work into making your mind into something different."

"Good for them," he says. "And good luck to them."

I'm about to release the headlock, but he actually holds on to my arm. It's less of a headlock now, more of an extremely friendly grip. We can walk this way.

"Can we take a walk around the Common before we get the trolley home?" he asks, like I'm his guardian or something instead of his pal.

His comrade in arms.

"I don't see why not," I say, and we cross the street into the busy, sunny, lively Common. "Rudi," I say, "you wouldn't really want them to change you all over like that, would you?"

He thinks for a bit. "Yeah, I would. I wouldn't mind at all, if they made me into somebody who was good at stuff. That would be okay. But most of all, I hope they can change me into somebody who isn't so scared. Because Morris, man, I am *scared*."

"We're all scared."

"Not Ivan."

"Okay, Ivan doesn't count."

We spend a solid hour doing nothing much as we walk around the Common like a married couple. In all our lives we have never used the Common as anything much more than a place to walk through on the way to someplace else, except when the Christmas lights were up.

"I love this place," Rudi says.

"Me, too," I say.

And any day now, we'll be leaving it all behind for a place, and a life, that couldn't be much farther away.

PART
TWO

CHAPTER SIX

Operation Overlord

In my head, in my mind and my dreams, I sit and watch. From my perch along the coast, this strange green salad of a place is manageable. I can see where the ocean I know meets this land that I never will know. It is a vision I can live with.

I am watching over all the guys. My guys, and whatever other guys, but mostly my guys. I can watch and keep everybody safe. Somehow.

The USS *Boston* is my home now. How much more perfect could it get? It's almost like I never left, right? The ship — a heavy cruiser — has practically got its own skyline, which could look like the regular Boston's skyline if only you squinted. Really, really hard.

That is, if you squinted and you were looking at it from a distance. Which I cannot do.

"Thinking about home already?"

I'm surprised but not startled by the voice up close to my ear. You get used to having people right behind you, beside you, on top of you in the Navy. The voice belongs to one of my new best friends, whose nickname is Huff. His full last name is Huffnagel, but unlike me, he seems like a guy who's been comfortable with the nickname thing for some time. He probably gave it to himself.

"We *are* home, remember?" I say.

"My home has grass and trees. I don't see any grass and trees here."

"Sailor," I say, "you lack imagination. Look at those mighty oaks directly above us." I point up at the big brute 8-inch guns stretching out just overhead from the turret. There are two forward turrets, each with three 55-foot guns protruding, and if they ever wanted to go at each other, they could swing around and be staring so close, the guys inside could exchange winks and wave greetings before blowing everybody to bits. I hope they never get that bored.

"Okay, they are mighty. But I think we'll be missing the greenery soon enough, if you want to be pretending those are trees."

I sigh. The wind whipping over you when you are out at sea is always strong enough to take a sigh right out of you like it never happened. Which is good, because I sense a lot of sighing over the next four years of my enlistment.

Four years. Four. I look at that same distance behind me, and I see a boy just leaving eighth grade. I look forward that same distance and I see . . . what?

Should I even try and look that far, considering everything?

"Yeah," I say. Then I sigh again. "I'll miss home."

Huff slaps me hard on the shoulder, harder than I used to get slapped, probably lighter than I will be getting slapped.

"But listen, Mo . . ."

I am Mo on this ship. I have never been Mo before. I am not the type to be called Mo. Nicknames come with the territory here. I sleep in a bunk — a rack — with one guy hovering about two feet above me and another two feet below. Getting along is probably better than fighting a nickname that is meant with all the best intentions no matter how stupid it might sound.

So I'm Mo now. A whole different somebody leading a whole different operation. This will just be the Mo part of my existence, in between the Morris part I came from and the Morris part I will return to.

"My man Mo," Huff says, "we need to get used to this. To learn to love it. Right? It's not the same as regular home life, so it does no good to compare it. This life is different, as different as we could get. Learn to love it, is what I think."

"So, what's to love?" I ask.

"Glad you asked."

Next thing I know, we are surrounded by boom.

"Boom," he says, as we walk around the cramped and dense munitions storage area deep within the ship. It's not a new place to me. We've all been introduced to every inch of this vessel. The space is chock-full of shells for the big guns up topside, smells of steel and oil and gunpowder, and as we walk up and down, Huff is touching, smelling, tasting every shell as if we have stumbled across some combination of God's own pastry kitchen and the arsenal of true love.

"Boom," I repeat back at him.

"Boom," he repeats back at my repeat.

"What's so special about all this, Huff?"

I have been walking along behind him, acting as if the two of us are on some kind of inspection tour. Only now he turns around and faces me. And it becomes unlike the usual inspection tours that happen in the Navy about every fifteen minutes of every day.

He goes right up to one of those impressive, deadly, not-that-pretty shells and nuzzles it.

"Why are you nuzzling that shell, Huff? It's pretty weird, and I'm not sure, but I'd be willing to bet it is against regulations."

He smells it really close, and it's pretty convincing. I

thought he was testing me, seeing if he could freak me, but now, no. He's in love.

"You ever felt like you had power before, Mo?"

I shrug. "I suppose," I say.

He's shaking his head at me.

"No?" I ask.

"No," he says. "Not like this. Look at you. Skinny. Young. Polite. You never had an ounce of real power in your life, and it shows from a mile away."

"Thanks. Now that you put it that way, I guess I'll just go lie down somewhere out of the way while the rest of you guys do the warring."

"Hey, it's not your fault. And don't get me wrong, I never had any, either, even though I'm sure that surprises you."

It doesn't. But like I said, best to get along.

"But brother, whatever was true up to now, it's all different. We got power, me and you."

"Except that people boss us around all day, every day, tell us where to be and when to be there and how to do every little thing and what is going to happen to us if we don't do every little thing just exactly the way we are told to do it."

Huff is staring at me now, all deadpan. Then, very dramatically, he kisses the nose of one of the shells. So dramatically, I'm actually a little uncomfortable.

"That stuff doesn't matter," he says. "This," he pats the shell, "matters a whole lot, Mo, because our country is in need, and we have answered the call, we have been handed some awesome power, and make no mistake, we are going to use it. Before this big adventure is over, we are going to unleash this stuff and we are going to change lives, and who would have said that about us, a couple of teenage nobodies, a year ago, huh?"

Huff's words continue zinging around the steel and brass that make up the interiors all round the ship. Words tend to do that in here. When they stop, I start.

"And end some."

"What?"

"Lives. If we use this stuff, we wind up ending some lives, right?"

"That's one view," he says.

There is something in Huff I have not encountered before. You might think from what he is saying that he is nothing but some bloodthirsty cowboy, but that would be incorrect.

"I don't want to kill anybody," Huff informs me. "And I don't plan to kill anybody."

"What are you gonna do with the big guns, then?"

"Blast 'em, of course. Smash things, destroy things, blow things up. Honest, Mo, I hope I don't kill anybody this whole war. 'Cause I feel the same way Muhammad

Ali feels. Like what he said, *I ain't got no quarrel with them Vietcong.* And that's true, I feel that way. I wouldn't know a Vietcong if he bit me —"

"He might yet."

"Well, *then* he gets killed. Until then, how I see my job is, I am here to end this war. And to do that I am gonna blast away, smash things, destroy things, just until we show 'em who's boss. That's how you win a fight, by showin' 'em who's boss."

He is back to over-loving the shell as he speaks.

"And this makes me boss, Mo. Me and you. We're bosses, like never before. I gotta admit, I cannot wait to fire them guns for real."

"Yeah," I say, "I kinda gather that."

"But I'm not here to kill anybody. That's for the Marines. We're just here to pound the daylights out of 'em, nice and simple."

"Simple. And nice."

"Exactly."

"If you say so, Huff."

"I say so."

And that is that, for now. Eventually, Huff and I and loads and loads of other guys here in the city of *Boston*, not to be confused with the city of Boston, have to hit the rack. We are supposed to sleep when we can, to be ready for the times when we can't.

Except that, during lots of the time when I'm supposed to sleep, I can't.

I hear Huff snoring in the rack across from me, and Rivera talking quietly in the rack below me. That's how you know when Rivera is sleeping, because he's talking. Awake, he's about the shut-uppest guy I have ever met, so I suppose that's why it all has to come out when he's asleep. I have a thought that maybe he stopped talking when he got on this ship and found himself stuck with the nickname Vera. But I wouldn't know for sure, because he won't say. Maybe he'll tell me in his sleep one night.

Which I would probably miss anyway, because I don't like to stay in my rack for very long. For starters, the nightmares are back. They're basically the nightmares I had before, where Rudi, Beck, Ivan, and I are all slaughtered in Vietnam. Only now they're higher-quality nightmares, after basic training and the war stories you get from every single person you meet in the military whether you want to hear them or not. My nightmares are now more graphic and better informed.

And it seems I have discovered a kind of claustrophobia I never knew I had. It's a strange relationship you have out here on a naval vessel in the middle of the ocean. It becomes an odd and unexpected outside/in thing. The topside of the ship is truly as outside as you could ever be in this world. The constant fierce wind and the spray, the insane distance of nothingness on the horizon and the sky being bigger than any universe I ever thought existed. That is the Navy I thought about, when I thought about the Navy.

But then you go inside. Belowdecks, downstairs, whatever you want to call it, and it all closes in on you. It's too hot. The air sits still and always carries a whiff of the one guy out of twelve hundred who needs a shower. The racks are close. The iron walls are close. It is a gigantic mother of a ship carrying a whole lot of little smallnesses within. It gets to me. It gets to me, and I get to *out*.

It's why I don't normally spend more than two consecutive hours sleeping before I go wandering. I don't know, honestly, if the new vastness of the ocean outside has made me more critical and uneasy, or if it is just the configuration of the ship, or the Navy itself that's done it. But I'm uneasy.

And then, of course, there's this: I can hardly keep a decent watch over my boys from inside, can I? What good am I asleep, or canned like Spam in the depths of the ship?

What if it happened, to any one of them, while I was sleeping?

So I walk around and around, sucking in the night air, watching for whatever's out there in the sweet black air. It takes an eternity for our ship to get over to the other side of the world in order to blow parts of that world to pieces. Weeks of quiet routine before we get to the real thing, which we know will be anything but quiet. Or routine.

I wish this part would last a little bit longer. But it can't. We've got a mission. I've got a mission.

And before long, after a lap and another lap of the ship, I wind up where I always wind up, staring up, aft of the ship. I am staring straight up, like a little boy, at the awesomeness of our two Terrier guided missiles sitting ready in their launchers.

And I know just exactly what Huff is talking about. He likes the big guns in their tanklike turrets, and I like our guided missiles, pointed and ready to do the business. Like nobody's business.

I feel the rush every time I see them. I feel something I never knew was in me before. I'm not about to nuzzle the Terriers, but I'm a lot closer to it than I ever would have expected.

CHAPTER SEVEN

Mission Statement

According to our mission, we would be having plenty of opportunities to fulfill Huff's dream of smashings.

The USS *Boston* is a heavy guided missile cruiser that has two primary jobs to do as part of Operation Sea Dragon. We are a kind of big brother escort to our smaller, faster, feistier little brothers like the *Sacramento*. And we are to provide heavy artillery support for our troops doing all the dirty hand-to-hand fighting in-country there in real honest-to-goodness Vietnam.

In-country is what they call that, the gritty land war. As opposed to off-coast, where I am. Makes me sound like a tourist by comparison, huh?

The second function, when you get right down to it, is the reason I am here.

I know my reason is unreasonable.

But that is, I think, the way a guy gets through a situation like this. You have to develop your own small crazy in order to cope with the big crazy that is war. No matter how right the fight, no matter draftee or short timer or lifer or whatever, the basic truth of a whole bunch of us guys over here trying our best, with all the machinery we have, to pulverize all their guys, and all of their guys using whatever means necessary to wipe out all of ours . . . well, it puts you in a constant state of mental somethingorother that you'd have to be crazy not to call crazy.

And so yes, this is my small crazy. In my head, I see myself, from my floating post here off the coast of what looks like a pretty lush garden, protecting my lifelong personal friends. That is my mission. They are there, on the ground, right now, and cannot see me for the distance and the foliage. But in my head and the eyes of my small crazy, I can see them. Because I am the overseer. As long as I am here off this coast, firing on my friends' enemies, we are all going to get through this and come home okay.

I believe that.

The United States Navy has its ideas about what my mission is, as it has pretty clear ideas about everything. And that's fine. They have trained me and conditioned me to do certain things with the very serious gear they have assembled for the purpose and, again, I say that's fine. I am an Aviation Electrician's Mate Third Class (AE3). Sounds a little sad, like my whole designation is just to be some kind of little buddy — third-class buddy, at that — to the real grown-up electricians on board. But I'm cool with that, as there are about a zillion miles of wiring, plus switches and sockets and transformers on a ship like this, so something minor is always going on the fritz. I get small repair jobs with instructions not to electrocute myself or anyone else. I even carry around a special, official Navy electrician's knife on my belt. The second blade is a screwdriver, while the longer one is a regular knifing knife, so just in case we get overrun by the enemy, I can give him a quick stabbing and then get back to changing a fuse, thereby fulfilling both of my main duties for my country.

But my duties are not the same thing as my mission. My mission is more my own thing. I don't think my personal sense of mission necessarily clashes with the Navy's mission, and as long as that is the case, everybody should manage just fine out of the deal.

As a matter of fact, I have trouble seeing how a guy like me — which is to say, a normal anybody guy like anybody — could manage the big, titanic, official US Navy, Walter Cronkite CBS Evening News–worthy mission without working directly on a small, important mission of his own. That kind of thing is what gets you fighting and keeps you fighting. I don't know how to stop the spread of Communism (or whatever that even really is, from what I can tell) throughout Southeast Asia. But I do believe I know how to look out for my guys. All four of us — I'm counting me, because we all need me to come home, too — out there somewhere. And okay, Beck is going to be in the sky mostly, more likely to be overseeing *my* safety, which is a comfort, because he's Beck. And Beck would hardly even need anybody's help in the air, on the ground, or in one of those Riverine boat operations that are in the thickest thick of it. But that changes nothing, anyway. I am overseeing the safety of my boys.

My mission. If I carry out my mission well, then the Navy gets what they need from me. They win. We win. The United States wins.

Communism loses. Sorry, Communism, but that's just how it has to go.

When we finally reach our destination, the country that's been scaring me out of my wits on the news every night for so long, I realize that as much as I thought I was prepared, I was not prepared.

The sky is alive. There is hardware and fire, noise, thunder, screech jet sounds and rumble deep enough to come right up through the Gulf of Tonkin waters and make all seventeen thousand tons of *Boston* hum beneath us. As I stare at the new world we are steaming into, it could not seem further removed from the peace of the world we steamed out of just a few weeks before.

"Thank God for violence, huh, Mo?"

It's a slap on my shoulder and a voice in my ear, only this time it is not Huff, it's Moses, who most certainly would have caught the nickname Mo if I hadn't stumbled into it first. I think the military nickname machine was stumped by this turn of events, because everyone seemed to fold and just reverted to calling him Moses. But since he said nobody had called him Moses since sixth grade, when a teacher tried it and he keyed MO into the hood of her car, you could make a case that Moses was now the nickname and Mo the proper full-time one.

Since we've been on board, I cannot think of three things Moses has said that I've agreed with. There is no good reason for me to like him.

I just do.

"Not so sure I'm with you on this one, Moses," I say. I have said this exact sentence to him at least seven times a day since the day I met him. But this is the first time I've said it while watching a US Air Force jet scorch low across the sky about a mile in shore, apparently launching whole flocks of grenades randomly in all directions.

"Come on, Mo," he says quite happily, "institutional, industrial-strength violence, baby — where would we be without it?"

I take a stab. "Home?"

"Exactly," he says. "I rest my case."

It's impossible for me to tell whether he thinks that explains itself to me, or if he just wants me to ask, but I don't care. I'm satisfied whenever his case rests.

But we don't have to agree on this: We are sailing into a *world* of violence here.

I know, it's a war. It should be no surprise.

I'm surprised anyway. And I'm not alone. It's dusk as our ship pulls close enough to the coast to finally, officially be considered part of the conflict. And as we approach the show, and the noises and the flashes and the projectiles and explosions, and even the smell of the world changes from salty sea mist to smoke and explosives and chemical burn, I am joined at the rail by my new collection of guys. My shipmates.

Moses is leaning heavily on my shoulder now, like we are a couple on a date watching a war movie on a gigantic drive-in screen. He is making small hungry noises.

Huff is there on my other shoulder, giving it perspective. "Holy smokes," he says, and he is about as right as he could be. We are looking at holy smokes.

The other guys I know from the racks all around me

are at my back now. We are all watching the same light show, which would be a thrill and a treat if the show was something other than what we all know it is. This is the real thing, killing, on a wide scale and with precision. US aircraft fly day and night over the coast, looking for movement of weapons and supplies, and when they see anything, they pick up the horn and call to the command center in Saigon and the center calls to the likes of us, or tanks, or, in this case, aircraft carriers. Jets, probably from the *Kitty Hawk* or *Enterprise*, stationed out in deeper water, are zooming everywhere, pounding the shore mercilessly.

Shells blast from cannons of ships already parked a little farther up the coast, soaring across the sky to land on vehicles, buildings, any structure along the shore. The sound, booming and screaming when the missiles launch, has an even bigger payback on land. The explosions look as if they are generated up out of the earth. Geysers of fire shoot straight up into the air in eighty-foot columns when the blast meets fuel and artillery. The sky gradually fills with spark and ash, smoke and chemicals, turning the fading daylight into grades of orange, blue, brown. From this distance it almost seems like there is no human presence in there at all, like we are just practicing blowing up inanimate stuff like with the fireworks on Jamaica Pond.

But we know better, because reconnaissance tells us so.

Bruce is here. We call him Bruise. He's the only one who actually gave himself his own nickname after coming on board. Normally, that isn't allowed, but his name was both so desperate and so hilarious, we had to let it stand. Bruise was trying to add a little bit of ruggedness to himself, before people's impressions formed and it was too late. Truth is, if Bruise punched with all his might, a banana would not bruise.

"Where do we even start?" says Bruise.

Rascal Cavaliere has an answer for him. It should be noted that Rascal has an answer for everybody, everywhere, always. "We don't," he says. "Looks like they've got everything covered here. Tell the old man to take a right, we'll make a beer run to Bangkok."

"Gotta earn it first, boys," Huff says. "Fight first, beer later."

We take in the scene for a while now, the chatter winding down to nothing. This is as big a part of our education, I figure, as anything they showed us in basic training.

Vera Rivera is behind me, too. I can only sense him, because his aim in this life appears to be to see and hear, not be seen, not be heard. Somehow, though, I always sense him.

But one of us is not looking, and we all know why. The last of our little family is still back at "The House." The House is the name we gave to our sleeping quarters, three racks against one wall, next to three racks on the other wall about an arm's length away. Not quite a room, and certainly not a house, it is the section of the ship, and therefore the war and the world, that has been set aside for us to live in for now. I think it's fair to say this family was formed pretty much as naturally as any other family gets formed — by being thrown in together to make the best of it.

And right now, back at The House, making the best of it, is our sixth family member. We call him Seven. Short for Seven Hands Vaughn. He has this small two-thirds-size practice guitar that he plays almost all the time, and he plays it so completely, it sounds indeed like there are seven hands working at it. Rascal came up with that. Rascal was very much on the ball there.

Seven is not with us because Seven has no interest at all in what is going on out there. Seven is in one way, at least, the exact opposite of me. He spends every last possible second of his Navy life back there in The House. If he could do his entire tour and never lay eyes on the country of Vietnam or the South China Sea, I believe he would be one happy guitar-playing boy. "Lemme know how it go" is what he normally says when anybody is leaving The House. He even has a little bottleneck slide guitar theme he plays when he says it, the high note wobbling away on the words *know* and *go*.

It's a good group. I like them very much, and am glad I've got them.

They will never be *the* group, though, will they?

CHAPTER EIGHT

The Business

Everybody stands watch, no matter what else his job is. Six hours on, six hours off, there is always watching to do, around the clock. I'm an electrician third class, and there is plenty for me to do on a ship this size. But not so much that I don't also do a lot of watching.

I wanted communications. That is what I should be doing, is communications. There is so much communications that happens in the Navy, it is a wonder we have any time left over to be blowing things up. On the *Boston* alone, there are scores of guys spending all day seated in front of these big blinking disks of screens, electronic and computerized systems that build up a picture of what is going on in the sea and on land all around us. The screens look like portholes, and they sort of are, in that they give a peek at what's outside.

But unlike old-fashioned portholes, these are insanely tricky to learn and to operate. Truth is, at this stage I wouldn't be up to the job, and we'd probably bump right into every other ship or sink our own boats if they gave me a shot at it.

Apparently, there are even more people who *want* to be in communications jobs than there are communications jobs, and so I am on a list, fixing coffeepots and stuff while I make my way. Meantime, I watch.

"Man, have you ever felt anything like this?" I ask, walking my little mini patrol along the starboard side of the ship with Moses. "I mean, humid is one thing . . ."

"Man, this ain't humid. This is *swimming*."

We have left our position just south of the demilitarized zone (DMZ), which is about a two-kilometer band stretching across the whole of the North and South Vietnamese border. Troops from either side aren't allowed in the zone, as if the land doesn't belong to either. It belongs to the war, I suppose.

Now we are looking at a whole 'nother country. North Vietnam. There are a couple of things that make these two places very different. One, North Vietnam, unlike South, has not invited us to be here. That's kind of important and changes the nature of things considerably for a ship floating off their waters. And two, my mission now is not to provide cover and protection for my boys fighting on the ground of South Vietnam. My mission now is to pound the bejesus out of somebody else's pals.

I feel like I have left my post. Like I have left them unprotected.

Until, suddenly, that thought gets blown right out of my mind.

The first shot sounds innocent enough, a boom, but muffled. I think first it's one of our side exploding something on the North Vietnamese. An instant later, though, and the reality hits home.

Bu-bhooom! A massive explosion, not more than fifty yards in front of us. A geyser of water shoots straight up out of the ocean. Then the muffled boom again, and again.

Bu-bhooom!

Sirens start blasting all over the ship. Guys appear out of nowhere and everywhere, running and climbing into positions and manning battle stations. Because the battle is on. My task in these situations is to run up to the big gun turrets and stand by along with a bunch of other guys, ready to be running ammo up the line.

The sound of our 8"/55 guns is something beyond belief. Again, they prepared us for this, but they didn't, they couldn't. I happen to be directly under one of the turrets when the boys start firing back, and I tell you, I have never been as terrified of anything in my life. You could combine *all* the terrors of my life to this point, and they would not add up to this.

And it is relentless.

Boom!   *B-B-B-B-B-BOOOM!*   *B-B-B-B-B-B-BOOOM!*

It's like a machine gun, only a million times the power, the sound, the size. Everything is faster and bigger and louder. Guys are shouting all over the place — it's chaos. Except that it isn't. Because we are trained for this. We are fighting men now, and whatever the fear and the shock and the adrenaline, we are here for this, and deep down nothing is getting in the way of our being here for exactly this. Our mission.

I am petrified. But I am not overwhelmed.

Within the first thirty seconds, I conclude that I am going to die here and now.

Thirty seconds later, when I find that I am not dead, I conclude other things.

I conclude that I am never going to die.

I conclude that I have never been more alive in my life.

I watch our shells trace across the sky, arc majestically, and come crashing down on the very skull of North Vietnam. I find myself yelling, bellowing, for the gunners to step it up. Pound them. Put them away. I don't even know what I'm looking at out there, but I'm suddenly gesturing, pointing out spots for them to target there on the distant unknowable shore. As if I know what I am doing. As if anybody would be heeding me even if I did.

That is adrenaline, I guess.

"Did I tell ya? Did I tell ya?" It's Huff, rushing up beside me, grabbing me as if he's going to toss me over the side, but just shaking me like a madman instead.

"You told me, Huff."

"Will I ever have to tell you again?"

"You won't. This is unbelievable."

"It doesn't get much better than this. To be young men, in the warm morning Asian air, pounding the stuffing out of the enemy? And they started it. Right?"

"They started it, Huff. We were just floating here, minding our own business."

Even as I am saying it, I am aware that this is, at best, an incomplete summary of events. We were floating here, minding our own business, with our hellacious firepower angled in a hostile way toward their country. Would I be so reasonable with them if they were likewise floating off Hyannis?

No.

But so what?

Then as I stare at the action, the real action comes

to me. I get a sharp shove at my side and look to find another sailor waiting to off-load a big shell on me.

"Resupply! Resupply!" I hear from above.

A supply line has formed, and we commence passing the heavy shells up the line to the gunners.

"I cannot wait to get my shot, boy, I tell ya," Huff says as I hand off to him. Huff is a gunner. But this is not his shift. He will get his turn. "I just want to blow stuff up, y'know. This is cool, but honest, that business down south of the DMZ, that's the stuff that's got my name on it. Blowing tunnels and bridges and supply lines right off the map, that's the stuff that's gonna show 'em who's boss, and nobody even needs to get hurt, am I right?"

What he means by nobody getting hurt is that tunnels and bridges and supply lines don't tend to shell you back. Here in the North, we are taking on the full forces of a country rather than pockets of resistance.

So he's not right. But again, do I care? Adrenaline says no.

"You're right, Huff."

From what I can tell, the enemy stopped firing in our direction quite some time ago. From the explosions and ongoing villages of fire we have created, it seems we got our man, and then some.

But we continue to pound the daylights out of them. We continue to pound, like we get paid by the artillery we use.

And I continue to watch, and my heart pounds every bit as hard as the big, bad 8"/55 guns that are making every other sound in the world meaningless and futile.

CHAPTER NINE

Burst First

It takes forever for mail to reach us. We, as a ship, have our own ZIP code and everything. But I suppose if you're nowhere near a post office, and your entire ZIP keeps moving up and down a strange coastline, you can hardly blame the mailman if he's not exactly popping 'em through the slot in the way you're used to.

When it does arrive, though, we have a kind of ritual. Like a bunch of squirrels with acorns, we all make our way back to The House, where we lie back and silently read out our mail, waiting for whoever is going to burst first. It never fails. You just can't help eventually sharing pieces of your mail out loud with the guys.

One of the good things I have learned from Navy life is that despite our backgrounds, there is a lot more in common between us than I had ever really thought about. First among those things is food. Everybody's mother asks about the food.

"'Are you getting greens?'" Moses reads to us, though he is doing equal parts laughing and reading so we have to listen hard. "'You know, son, that you will never be fed greens the way you were in this house here, so you are going to have to make sure you get your hands on whatever greens you can find. And please, don't let them tell you that that ol' iceberg lettuce is any kind of greens because that is pure nonsense. Shouldn't even call them greens, they should call them whites. And speaking of whites to look out for . . .'" The rest of the letter is omitted. Not to protect anybody's sensitive ears, but because Moses is now laughing so far beyond his ability to form words, he may not ever get back. He's in the rack above me, and when he laughs himself right out of that rack, I snatch the letter out of his hand as he flies by. He lies flat on his back looking up as I hold it, but he just keeps laughing without making any effort to get it back.

I hand it to him, unable to keep from laughing myself, though I haven't read a word. You don't read another guy's mail unless he clearly tells you to.

"'Scurvy!'" Seven reads out, from his own mom. "'You do know about scurvy, don't you? It is a disease that the Navy is famous for because of their inadequate food, so unless you want to come back to me with horrible bandy legs and bendy bones, you make sure you get vitamin C, and A, and D, and all the sunshine you can manage.'"

This time it's the audience that makes the reading impossible. Everybody roars at the notion of Seven getting sunshine. Then he puts down his letter, picks up his guitar, and starts howling his way through Cream's "Sunshine of Your Love."

"'You're all the sunshine I need, Ma,'" he sings, really mangling the original lyrics. But hey, it's his mom.

Rascal has the biggest stack of letters. He claims they are all from heartbroken girls.

"Okay," Huff says, "read us one. Any one."

"Cost ya a buck," Rascal says.

"What?" Huff says. "Don't be a dope. We're all reading."

"You ain't readin' what I'm readin'. A buck. Guaranteed satisfaction, or your money back."

"I could just lie and say I was not satisfied and you'd never know."

"I sleep two and a half feet away. I'll know."

We laugh a lot at letter time.

There are also great fat silences that seem to come over all of us at exactly the same time. I don't know how that happens.

Right now the place goes silent while the guys read whatever private stuff they've got. Me, I'm reading Rudi.

DEAR MORRIS,

How hard is the war going to be if even your own guys scream and shout at you all day long? The sergeant screams so much and so close up to me, it feels like it is always raining on my face.

Sorry, how are you, Morris?

I'm scared all the time though maybe not as much as you might expect. Are you scared? I've been hearing a lot about the Navy. The Marines talk about the Navy a real lot. They say yours is the easy war and the safe war. That we do all the dangerous stuff while you sailors mostly go fishing and work on your tans. Then there's all that other stuff that I can't even repeat that they say about sailors. Do you think all that is true? About you having an easier war than me? Does it feel like that to you?

Here's what I mean about being not as scared as maybe you'd of thought I might be. The surprise thing is, I think I fit in here. I know, isn't that crazy? All those years and years of never fitting into anything that didn't have you and Ivan and Beck making sure I fit and even then never being a really good fit anyway, let's be honest. Then I get this letter telling me I now belong to a whole new something and it's a something that scares me into wetting my pants. Remember that? I am sure that you do. But then comes the funny part and it is that I settle into the Marines real quick. Like from the first day of basic training. I like the way the days are all put together for you so you don't have to worry about where to be or what to do. I like the idea that we have a big important something that we gotta do. I like the idea that the kind of jobs you get in the Marines mean it is kinda clear whether you get it right or wrong without a lot of talking or thinking about it. I mean you shoot at a guy, you can sorta tell if you got it right, right?

And here is an important something, Morris, that I probably wouldn't even tell the guys here because I don't want them to think I am crazy, at least not so soon. I found out I really like to be told what to do. I even like to be screamed what to do if that is what they think they need to do.

The Marines don't complicate things for me which pretty much everybody else always does. It is like they know me.

I hope your tan is doing well (I am joking there) and that you are not missing home too bad.

Your very good friend,
PFC Rudi

"What's so funny?" Bruise asks.

I am not even aware of laughing.

"He fits," I say, and I'm aware of shaking my head in wonder.

"Who fits where?"

"My pal from home, Rudi. Starting to look like he's a pretty snug fit with the US Marine Corps."

"Is he mentally defective?" Moses asks, quite seriously, probably reasonably.

"No," I snap. "He's just a natural-born Marine."

"That's a yes, then."

Everybody's laughing. They are laughing because it was a funny line.

I'm not laughing. Stupidest, strangest thing ever, but all of a sudden I'm all choked up. Who could believe it?

Next thing I know, I'm standing, squared up in front of Moses's rack.

"You gotta take that back, Moses," I say.

And just like that, nobody's laughing anymore.

Moses, back lying comfortably in his rack, stops reading his letter, holds it flat to his chest. He looks at me and speaks in an odd-sounding way, a little like a question and a lot like a form of pity. "Sit down, Mo."

As he is in the rack above me, and we are eye-to-eye, that should be good advice. I would very much like to just lie back down.

"I will be very happy to sit down, after you take back what you said about my friend."

One by one, each of the guys swings around to a sitting position in his rack. Except Moses.

"You can't be serious," he says.

"I think I can." I'm fighting myself not to tremble too obviously. It's the only fight I am truly up to here. And I think I'm even losing this one. "You can't say stuff like that about a guy's friend when you don't even know him."

I sound crazy. Even to me I sound crazy. But there is this great gulf between what I can rationally think and what is flopping around in my gut. And my gut is feeling this overwhelming need to protect and defend Rudi. To make sure that he isn't taking any more guff off of anybody than he already has, than he already has to.

Especially about his intelligence.

Moses wounded *me*, is what he did. Because he made me feel like Rudi was unprotected, let down by me, personally. I was failing in my mission already.

Even if it sounds like Rudi needs less protection than I do right now.

"You going to take it back, Moses?"

He gives it just a little bit of thought.

"Nah, I don't think so."

"Then I'm going to have to call you outside."

Basically, the same sound comes out of every guy in The House, including me, including Moses. A groan.

"Just take it back, Moses" is one popular sentiment.

"Just let it go, Mo" is the other one.

But both perfectly reasonable options lose, and I find myself following Moses out of The House, through the passageway, and up to the next deck. We don't even get topside, since that's not where the fighting goes on. It became common knowledge almost as soon as we boarded ship that the private place for sorting out differences of opinion is on the gun deck below topside, right underneath the turret, where munitions are stored and not much else happens with the ample space. I follow Moses through hatches and up ladders as if I were his apprentice.

We reach the empty space and stand opposite each other. I assume the position, arms up, fists curled in, almost like I am ready to punch myself. I have no idea where I learned this stance.

It's possible I have never felt stupider in my whole life.

I don't stand a chance, and it would be very difficult for me to put into words what I might hope to achieve. I would bet that nobody on the entire ship would vote for this to happen, other than the utter complete sickos who just love blood for blood's sake. For his part, Moses's face shows no hint of any kind of pleasure in this.

And yet. Somewhere deep inside, where common sense cannot reach, I feel noble about this.

Until the punch.

Moses says, "Okay?" like he's asking permission.

I nod, and his hands are so quick that as I nod I actually nod my nose right into his straight snapper of a right hand.

I go down. My knees buckle and I fall forward, making things even more pathetic by bashing my mouth on Moses's knee on my way down. My arms don't feel right, don't do the job of getting me up off the floor. I can feel the warm blood pooling up behind my wiggly bottom front teeth. I manage eventually to stagger to my feet and find Moses politely waiting for me. I mimic his approach and say, "Okay?"

He nods, then punches me hard enough this time that, though I attempt to fall forward, I find myself sitting on my butt about six feet from where I started, looking up at my puncher. Then there is a gap. There are blackout conditions.

Then I am topside, at the rail, the wonderful, wonderful life-saving sea breeze blowing consciousness into me from the top down.

"You're a good boy, Mo," comes the voice right at my ear.

I turn to see Moses's face right in my face. Because he is holding me up. My arm is around his shoulders, and he is dabbing at my lip with a wet and ruined handkerchief.

"Does that mean I win?" I say, smiling and splitting the lip a little more open.

"You are a good boy, and a great friend to that jarhead, leatherneck, simpleton of a moron Marine idiot pal of yours."

He lays a big wide smile on me, one that does not have so much as a dent in it.

"Am I going to have to teach you another lesson?" I say. I'm at my most menacing, which is not wildly menacing at the best of times. But the truth is, the words feel fine now.

"Now, now, Mo, you know that violence never solved anything."

I'm wobbly, but not so bad I can't handle that one.

"Then what happened to my face?"

"We'll call that *friendly fire*. Very different thing. It's *real* violence that never solved anything."

"You don't believe that, Moses."

He laughs. "Nah. That was just a test to see if you had a concussion. Violence solves everything, man. That's why we're here."

I shake my head gently. I see things a lot differently from how Moses sees them. I always have, always will.

But I know I want him right beside me every single day until they send me home.

CHAPTER TEN

Cherry Bomb
Jamaica Pond

It always shocked me.

No matter how many consecutive Fourth of Julys we'd come here and do exactly the same thing. No matter how many consecutive years we took the green line to Park Street and then made the nervous walk over to the North End to purchase the illegal fireworks. I knew weeks in advance — certainly by, say, June 21 — what was going to happen and what it was going to sound like.

Still, it shocked me. Every time.

Cherry bombs, M-80s, bottle rockets, Roman candles, everything we could scrape up the money for was part of our arsenal. Then we would bring craft to float out on the pond and attack. Ivan, who only cared about the boom-boom element, just brought a copy of the *Globe* and folded boats out of the newspaper. Sometimes he didn't even bother with the folding, just balling a sheet up and telling us to use our imaginations as we fired away. Rudi usually managed to come up with something half-shipwrecked already, since he shopped in people's trash cans. Beck, also working the reasonable/economical side of things since we were going to destroy these things anyway, hand made a couple of boats out of scraps of whatever he found at home. His boats looked better than real boats and sometimes didn't even sink when we had done our worst.

Me, I always bought a Revell model kit special and slaved over the details, insignia, whatever, until the vapors from the glue made me fall out of the chair. The boats I brought were always as perfect as I could get them.

It was stupid, I know, but it felt right to me. There was always some little-boy part of me that just thought they deserved a certain respect, a fighting chance, if we were going to unleash all our firepower on them.

I never explained that to the guys. I know that Ivan, for one, would have floated me out on a boat and shot bottle rockets at me all day if I tried to explain my *feelings*.

I just never enjoyed the explosions much. I would spend 364 days every year convincing myself that that wasn't so, and then one day jumping out of my skin with shock and the wrong kind of surprise all over again. I always wanted to be there, because I never liked the guys doing things without me. Especially things that had become part of our traditions. But it got to be hard.

And then there were those nightmares.

They started coming pretty regularly the summer between junior and senior years. The news from the war was unavoidable, and in the daytime it would bleed into my head. At night, it would all start churning and bubbling in there, and the explosions would start, and all of us would die. Again. Again.

"I was thinking, maybe we don't need to bomb the boats on the pond this year," Beck said when it was nearing time for our North End rearmament.

We were walking around the pond, just walking around the footpath that circles it, walking to nowhere, which we did a lot of on good summer days.

I was surprised by this but made an effort not to seem like it.

"Huh?" I said casually. "What? Why?"

Beck is not the type to laugh outright in a guy's face, no matter how dumb the guy's being. Instead, he does this kind of relaxed semi-smile where one side of his top lip curls up and he lets his mouth hang open. You'd almost wish he would just laugh at you.

"Come on, Morris. It was pretty obvious by last year that you weren't getting much fun out of it. Now I figure the fact that you tell us about your explosive and tragic nightmares *every single day* probably has some meaning."

Every single day?

"Every single day?"

"Every single day."

"I didn't think I was telling it every single day."

"What did you think, that you were putting on a brave face or something?"

I had to consider.

"Yes. Actually, I did think that."

"Sorry, man. No brave face. Do you even have one of those?"

As we approached the boathouse, we ran into Rudi and Ivan, who were hiring out a rowboat for an hour. Rudi never seems to work out that this always winds up with him mysteriously falling into the water at some point, followed by Ivan laughing so helplessly, he only manages to save Rudi — who can only stay afloat so long — at just about the moment of drowning death.

"I think we're going to skip the bombing of the fleet on the Fourth this year," Beck said to them.

"What?" Rudi said. He got quite flustered at this tipping of the annual rhythm of the calendar, as if someone had suddenly canceled, say, August. He looked nervously back and forth between Beck and Ivan.

"It's just, with everything going on, and the night-mares and everything . . . Morris doesn't have any fun. So I thought we'd just skip it this time around. Maybe things'll be better next year."

Then it was Ivan's turn to look perplexed. He stared at Beck, head tilted, trying to make it make sense. He never quite achieved that.

"No," Ivan said firmly. "Request denied. Stuff needs to be blown up."

"Right," said Rudi, finally exhaling.

"Rudi?" Beck said, gesturing toward me.

I must have had my famously un-brave face on, because at the sight of me, Rudi looked like his dog had just died.

"Ah, I suppose," he said.

"Maybe we'll go to the Sox game this year for a change. They're about a million games out, there will be about a million tickets available. We can probably sneak in for nothing anyway."

Rudi brightened.

Ivan did not.

"Request denied," he said, more emphatically. "I told you, stuff needs to be blown up. *Somebody's* got to do it."

"Then I guess you'll need to do it alone," Beck said.

He had to know this would cut very little ice with Ivan.

"Then I'll do it alone," he said. He turned, tugging Rudi by the shirt down the dock toward the rowboats. Halfway down, he spun around again in our direction. "You guys are still making me boats, though, right? I can't do everything for you."

For *us*.

I laughed at him, because he was just being so totally Ivan about it all.

"I'll make you a boat," I said.

Beck, less amused by Ivan, didn't answer.

Just as they were getting into the boat, Beck shouted down, "Rudi? You do know he's going to dump you into the water, right?"

Rudi was actually offended by this suggestion.

"No," he shouted back. "I don't know that. Why would I know that? Why would he do that?"

Stepping into the boat, Ivan broke already into the laugh, so loud and hard he very well might not be able to rescue Rudi when the time came.

CHAPTER ELEVEN

History

The *Boston* has been around for a while. Commissioned in 1943, it served extensively in the Pacific in World War II. It received ten battle stars for the action it saw there. We don't have any stars here yet, and I'm okay if we don't get any. I like it quiet. And the ship, when it's quiet, holds the most peaceful kind of quiet I have found anywhere.

I have slept all I want to sleep, and I get up to go on my walk. Once up top I find just a suggestion of daylight that won't really be here for another hour and a half. The already saturated air is promising yet another muggy long day off the Vietnam coast. Even with the breezes we get out here some distance from the land, this can get heavy. There are some guys on this ship I have still never seen wearing a shirt, and I believe if the temperature ever dips below ninety degrees again I'm going to need a sweater.

I can only imagine how brutal it is for the guys in-country.

We are back just south of the DMZ again, support-ing the ground troops who call in a request to take out a tank or a convoy or a munitions depot, and big-buddying the *Sacramento* and the rest of the Seventh Fleet. *Sacramento* was alongside us yesterday, and I suppose you could say that like a lot of big brother–little brother deals, it's not completely even. They were restock-ing us with the big beefy shells we use to pound the senses out of our land targets. The support ships, bat-tleships, are faster than the cruisers, and do a lot of the running back and forth to support us. Like sending the little kid off to get snacks while we sit with our feet up watching TV. If your idea of TV is bombardment.

We are in good company this morning. One of the fun and surprising parts about living on a warship is that every morning you wake up and the whole place could have changed, with new buildings, new neighbor-hoods brought in overnight. Running just ahead of us, with the same angle on the coast, is the Australian guided missile destroyer *Hobart*. I do make an effort not to get all big-kid about this stuff, but the *Hobart* is a big brute of a thing, a lot like us, and together we make a sight, like a couple of burly mean and feisty brothers who could take on the world and anybody's navy. Right now we're lying about a kilometer off the coast of Cua Viet, which is about as north as you can get in South Vietnam. We float, in low light, growling softly, and I would have to say if I were the enemy, I would not be resting easily.

Also new to the neighborhood this morning are two swift boats, PCF-12 and PCF-19, which are fast becoming famous around here for completely menacing the enemy up and down the coast and deep into the rivers. They are a lot smaller than the cruisers, and faster than pretty much anything else around, so their game is mostly mayhem. The neighborhood is loaded this morning.

"Hey," Huff calls down as I pass by beneath his turret.

He is at his battle station and smiling like a nut, so it must be time for work.

"What's up?" I say when I climb up and take in the view from his deck.

"We're about to rock," he says, very excited.

"I'm happy for you."

"Be happy for yourself and stay to watch. Get up here behind me."

So I stay and get behind him. I work my molded wax earplugs into my ears and brace myself.

There is no bracing yourself for this.

B-boom b-boom, b-boom b-boom, b-boom b-boom, the cannons go off in their two-at-a-time, no-pause-for-breath assault. There is nothing on earth to compare with this sensation, especially from right behind it. The shells soar high into the air, and the explosions even one klick — that's a kilometer — away feel like they are happening right under my feet. I can't resist the impulse to keep looking at my feet, checking, I guess, that the ship is going to hold under me. I look back out, as the relentless pounding continues, and follow the trajectory, the beautiful perfect arc, of a shell I can focus on. When it lands, the entire sky looks like a screen that is projecting a movie of pure fire. We've hit a fuel depot for sure.

Shells begin coming back out our way. Booms get closer, and holes appear in the ocean, followed by eruptions of water fifty feet high. It is reminding me of Jamaica Pond and the Fourth of July. It is so similar — and also very, very different. I am as scared as I have ever been. I am as thrilled as I have ever been. Scared and thrilled are sensations I used to think I understood.

I wonder where my buddies are. I wonder, even, if we could be blowing them up ourselves. How are you supposed to be sure?

Every man on board is up and running around now. Battle stations, support stations. Rascal comes up and yanks me by the shirt.

"What you think, this is some kind of shoot 'em up game? You ain't on Nantasket Beach today, pal. We got work to do."

Rascal is the real electrician around here, and I am his flunky. We are required to answer every call for electrical work, and when things get hot all over the way they are now, we're not supposed to wait for calls. We rush around from station to station making sure all the electricals are functioning — which half the time they aren't.

"It has hit the *fan* this morning, eh, Mo?" Rascal says.

I still have my earplugs in, but everything in the world cuts through them now. Everything in this world.

"It sure has," I say. Rascal is excited, like everybody else. The *Hobart* is firing as fast as we are. The swift boats are racing around, off in the distance now, and it appears suddenly like they are in a fight all their own. Something is hovering there, the lights appearing, cutting out, appearing again. They have aircraft of some kind engaging them, and this I have not seen before.

I'm running up the ladder toward the control room, right behind Rascal. I'm watching everything, ducking from everything, not looking where I'm going. I smash my shin as I stumble on the steel rungs. I scream as my shin feels like shattering glass. But I keep running.

"Vera is frozen, man."

"What?" I say. Now I'm trying to run and watch the action and duck and rub my shin, all at the same time. It would be a good time to be an octopus.

"Vera, man. Rivera. He froze. Wouldn't answer the bell. Stayed in his rack. Nobody could move him. He's gonna get some serious grief coming his way when this is over."

One of the early lessons you learn in this operation is, you have to answer the bell. You have to, have to, have to answer the bell. Unless you're already dead. Then you're allowed to be a little bit late, but then, still, dead, answer the bell. You do not let your mates down, no matter what. Vera's main job is just domestic stuff, kitchen and laundry and such. But like everybody, he has duties in battle as well. He's a sailor, a soldier, a warrior. No excuses.

We are just to the top deck, nearing the control room, when it all changes again. For the first time, I feel bullets.

You feel them. Whether they hit you or not, you feel them. Like evil, large, lethal mosquitoes, you feel them buzzing all over, and it doesn't matter how hard the surface is, you *hit* the deck.

"Holy smokes," Rascal says as he launches himself at the deck.

I throw myself down with all the force of one of the rockets. I smash both elbows, and they feel the same metallic zing as my shin.

There are more aircraft now, and it is *us* under attack. There are small explosions, and I cannot believe I now think of these as small.

But I do. Because off in the distance I hear a mother of an explosion.

Smoke, big smoke, is puffing up off the *Hobart*.

Rascal and I scramble our way into the control room. The Officer of the Deck is hollering into the radio, and his assistant is relaying orders to all the different battle stations. The big guns continue to pummel the land targets, but the furious action has turned to the antiaircraft guns.

"American!" the OOD shouts.

"Negative!" I hear the response come back. "There is no American aircraft activity in the area. Deploy antiaircraft fire. Fire!"

"Fire!" the OOD shouts.

"Fire!" his man shouts into his microphone.

And they fire. It is now official and total mayhem. There is firefighting of all manner, in all directions. The antiaircraft guns are blasting away at several times the rate of the cannons, following the aircraft across the sky.

The OOD continues with headquarters. "Have we got confirmation?"

"Negative. There is no American activity within that sector. All activity has been suspended in order to isolate the problem. There is no, repeat, *no* friendly activity in the area."

I almost laugh. This is the truest thing I've heard anyone say since I joined the Navy.

There is no friendly activity in the area.

As those words come out, there are two almighty explosions. The first is off in the distance, but there's no doubt something severe has happened.

The second is closer to home.

The entire ship shudders, then tilts, and everyone is thrown to the deck. I can see smoke rolling up over the glass where the OOD had been surveying the action. He scrambles back to his feet, shouting into the phone, "Sir, we have been hit. We have identified, in the darkness, one hovering aircraft, rotating blade, gunship. And two jets, possibly F-104, F-2. We've been struck by rocket fire."

We hear the distinctive sound of jet engines shrinking into the distance. Our guns continue firing for a while, while smoke and fire lap up from a section at the front of the ship. I get up to the window in time to see a shocking sight. PCF-19 goes down so quickly, there's a splash, a plume of water at the end of it like off the tail of a diving whale. Whoever it was, they just sent one of our swift boats swiftly to the bottom of the South China Sea.

The *Hobart* has taken a hit like ours. The sun is coming up now over a scene of carnage. All guns cease, and it's as if we are all punch-drunk, standing, uncomprehending.

We've taken a beating.

I thought the American military never, ever lost. That's what I was taught my whole life. That's what I believed, right up 'til this minute.

"What are you two doing here?" the OOD screams at me and Rascal, finally noticing us.

Startled, Rascal regroups. "Electricians, sir. Here to check all is functioning. Properly."

"All is functioning properly here! I suggest you go and check the functionality down *there*." He points in the direction of flames toward the bow of the ship.

We scramble.

CHAPTER TWELVE

Life and Death

Fragments recovered from the rocket attacks on the ships indicated these were friendly fire attacks. Nobody has been able to put two plus two plus two together to find out who was there firing at us and why it happened.

Two Australian seamen from HMAS *Hobart* were killed. Seven more wounded.

Five American seamen from the swift boat PCF-19 died. Two were injured.

We got off easy. Nobody got killed, injuries were not even worth mentioning. Or at least by military standards they were not worth mentioning.

So why am I shaking so much?

Every time I think I have the experience to make some sense of all this, I am shocked all over again. I thought I knew war and shooting and danger and adventure, but no, I didn't, and I don't. See, there is a big fat difference between being taught to shoot at targets in training and doing the real thing in action. There is a difference between being told about injury and death and fear and all the well-known nonsense of battle, and feeling it.

And more to the point, there is a whopping great difference between dishing all this stuff out and being on the receiving end of it. Sounds like simple common sense, right?

Then why are even my eyelids trembling, not even blinking, but dried and petrified like they will never close again?

I know why. Because the war, the power of it, the wicked reality of the death-and-dismemberment aspect, are coming my way now.

And what do we get for our troubles? We get a vacation. We get to go home. USS *Boston* is taking me to the port of Boston just when I need it most. I could kiss them both.

We are to lick our wounds, repair our holes (just a scratch, everybody keeps saying, just a scratch). Our "holes" are a fairly mangled bridge area, a radar tower compromised to the point of dysfunction, and a lot of twisted and burned structural material across the ship's once handsome nose. While we get all that cosmetic upgrading, we will also receive a refit. We are to go from "Guided Missile Heavy Cruiser" to "Heavy Cruiser, Attack."

It seemed like we were already a heavy cruiser, and attack was our specialty. But what do I know?

What it means, really, is that our Terrier missiles are being decommissioned. It is all moving so fast. The Terriers, those impressive, hot killer rockets that first caught my attention at the aft end of the ship, have gone from latest thing to yesterday's news before our very eyes. The Navy has decided technology has passed the Terriers by and they are now obsolete. To me they look just as murderous and handsome as they did yesterday.

I know it's stupid, but I'm going to miss them.

I'm standing, like I did on the trip over, in the middle of the night as we steam through the endless open sea. It's breezy and warm and you can definitely tell the difference sailing home west as opposed to sailing to war east.

Or it could just be the smell of home.

There is no one around as I look up admiring the Terriers.

Then there's someone.

"Why don't you never sleep, man?"

I nearly fling myself overboard with fright. It's Vera, and it's one of the few times I've seen him out and about without an officer right on his back shouting and bullying him into it. He's one of those people, Vera, who makes you know how sad he is just by walking by. Not that he's a drag or anything, because really he never has a bad word for anybody, and if any one of us, anyone who is not a superior officer, asks for anything, he's right there with whatever. He's just . . . you know that look a person gets when they're really sick but they don't know what they've got? Vera wears that look all the time.

"I sleep," I say, exaggerating only a little. Truth is, I sleep a little bit less every week as time goes by.

"Not much," he says. "I know. You don't think I know?"

Somehow, you gotta know he knows.

"I worry," I say.

"Everybody worries," he says.

Probably he worries even more than I do. He got himself in a lot of trouble by not showing up for the war the night we got hit. He got punishments, but not as much as he could have. Skipping the actual battle parts of a war is about the most serious thing you can do in the service, but because the officer in charge either knew just what he was doing or knew nothing at all, Vera was punished with restriction to quarters. That's like sentencing a glutton to pizza and ice cream. But he got some leniency because it turned out he got sick and that's why he missed the big game. Lucky for him, right?

By the time they came to mop the floor with his butt, there was a lot more mopping to do, since he had decorated the whole House with vomit.

We all did the natural thing and mocked the guy mercilessly. We even braved the stench as Vera was forced to sponge down the walls until he puked even more and could not keep up with his own production.

He kept scrubbing until he passed out, with his mates' laughter still ringing in his ears.

Turns out the whole sickness thing was job related.

Seven Hands Vaughn told me later. Vera drank himself some bleach.

"You'd be a little nuts not to worry," I say.

"What do you worry about? Aside from the obvious stuff like getting blown up and drowning and all."

"My pals," I say, because even though this might seem quick to be answering so truly to somebody, Vera feels like a guy I could be friends with. Like if he wasn't so miserable he'd be great company, if that makes any sense. "I came over with three friends, and they are out there someplace, in-country. One guy, Rudi, got drafted into the Marines. And we kind of had a pledge, if one guy was drafted — especially if it was Rudi — we were all joining. I kind of feel like, from the ship, it's my job to look out for them."

I shrug, the way you do when your words come out and they float there stupid on the breeze and you're not sure they mean anything to anybody else.

Vera gives me a solidarity shrug.

I go on. "I imagine that when we fire our guns, we're shooting down the guys who're about to shoot down my guys. And I hope that we're not actually shooting down my guys along with them."

"The ol' friendly fire," Vera says with a snarly smile.

"The ol' friendly fire," I say.

We walk past the tall Terrier missiles, still pointed and baring their teeth in the direction of the Vietcong. We walk to the very back of the ship, to the rail above the churning water behind us.

"I imagine when we're firing our guns," Vera says, staring way, way off over the water, "that we're shooting my dad, over and over again. I worry that we keep missing him."

I face straight out to sea, just the way he does. But my eyes dart in my skull, side-to-side-to-side, pinball-like. I think he senses my discomfort and my need for a bit of explanation.

"He's a big man in the Marine Corps, my father. A colonel."

"Wow."

"Yeah, wow. He wanted me to join the Marines. I wanted no part of the Marines, or this stinking war at all. But my family . . . we're a big family, family is everything to us. And we go back, in the military. Uncles, cousins, everybody. Even the girls. Couldn't look nobody in the eyes ever again if I tried to stay out of it. Big shame."

"So you joined the Navy," I say helpfully. "Cool."

"Yeah, cool. Very impressed, my dad. The Nancy Navy, he called it. The Floating Fairies."

"Ouch."

"Ouch," he says, finding a new lower level of sad that I didn't think would be possible. "He called me Vera way before you guys did."

The way the water kicks up in our wake, it reminds me of films I used to see, of women water-skiing in fancy ridiculous Hollywood musicals. And then I'm thinking of World War II films, with PT boats cutting up the waters and sinking German U-boats and everybody being comrades in arms and knowing which side of everything was the right side and being sure to be on that side. Everybody always had great teeth in all those films. Vera has great teeth, and I'm forcing myself to think these things, because, I realize, I don't think I want to think about what Vera wants me to think about.

"I was a great shot," he says after apparently too much of all that Hollywood. "In basic training. Every type of gun they let me shoot — rifle, the cannons, antiaircraft, whatever they gave me — I could shoot the eyebrows off a fly a mile away. Must be in the blood, the Rivera genes."

"That's great," I say.

"Yeah, great. And I swore I was gonna come over here and shoot my father's eyes out. I was gonna make sure I knew where he was all the time and I was gonna shoot that way. Problem is, I think I said so out loud a few times."

"That explains the laundry duty."

"I believe my dad was scared of me, so he fixed things."

"Is that likely?"

"Likely? Did you know before you got here that they were actually gonna make us sing 'Anchors Aweigh'?"

"No, sir," I say, shaking my head vigorously and laughing. "I thought it was a joke song, from cartoons or something."

"Exactly. Now guess what. I can't stop. The song, it spins in my head night and day and day and night and I can't stop it. It plays at the same time with the Marines' hymn, 'From the Halls of Montezuma' — and I mean AT THE SAME TIME, with the words twisting and snaking in and all over each other. I'm not kidding you, man. It doesn't ever stop."

He turns and locks my eyes with his, right up scary close.

"My dad used to come in my room and sing that song in my ear while I was sleeping. Night after night. To make me into what he wanted me to be. And not what he didn't want me to be, you know what I mean? I would wake up, all sweating, that song in my head, but nobody there. I could smell him, though. Just me, there, alone, shaking, with his scent and his song, but no Dad. I *knew*, from his smell, he was there just a minute ago. Scent of Dad, but no Dad."

I get more of a chill now than from anything I have seen or heard yet in this war.

"That's . . . ah. Wow, man. No offense, but I don't think I'd give you a gun, either. I think the Navy's probably right about that at least."

Another first: Vera laughs. That's a relief. It feels like something is opening, so I step on in. "Why are you talking to me now so much, Vera? After all the not talking you've done all this time?"

His tensed-up features melt some to a real, soft, and hopeful smile. He looks like a kid.

"'Cause I been watching you, Mo. You're a good one. You're the real thing, aren't ya? And I need a friend."

It seems like a simple enough thing. It seems like the kind of thing that would happen to a person lots of times over the course of a life. But I cannot think of one time, even as a little boy, when somebody came right out and asked me if I would be their friend.

And here and now, in war and all. In the middle of the night and all. Facing off the stern of a great warship, the wind at our backs, the smell of the sea all around, the roll of the deck beneath our feet. It seems like the easiest answer in the world. Why not?

I try the easy way first, the *man* way.

"We're all your friends, Vera," I say. "All the guys."

He shakes his head. The smile remains.

"I mean a real friend. I don't think I have ever, once, had a real, true friend. And everyone should have one real, true friend before he dies, don't you think?"

It seems, again, like the simplest answer. Doesn't it seem like the simplest answer?

I give him the simplest answer.

Because I'm his friend.

"Yes," I say. "Of course."

But maybe if I was a better friend, I would have listened more closely, and I would have *heard*.

He's too quick for my mind to even contemplate his mind.

With the strength and speed and skill of a gymnast, and still with that angel's smile on his face, he is off.

He grabs the rail, flips over, and dismounts, throwing himself out and into the white and wild churning water below.

My new friend flies.

CHAPTER THIRTEEN

Home Again Home

In basic training they told us we could expect to learn something new every day in the Navy. Here is something I learned: In the military, in war, you make friends just like that. And you lose them again, just like that.

I raised the alarm. We tried to find him.

But we never did.

It's kind of funny that we receive our next shipment of mail just before we're due to arrive in Boston. In no time we're going to be face-to-face with most of the people who wrote us the letters, and so maybe we should save them and have them read to us by the authors.

Pretty funny, huh?

All the guys from The House are sitting in mess, our food in front of us, our mail in hand.

Here's another funny thing: We lost our quietest guy, and somehow The House got quieter.

The plan was to take the mail to dinner, read out loud, mock each other, throw food and be stupid, without thinking any of the thoughts that are likely to make our trip ashore less fun than it should be.

Instead, we read to ourselves. We eat like birds, and I don't mean seagulls. Seven Hands plucks away at something that haunts, that I have never heard but that feels like I have known it all my life.

I have a letter from Beck.

Hello Lucky,

You are welcome. Even though I am so jealous I could puke, you are welcome anyway. Everyone is talking about what happened to you boys and how your reward was a trip back to Boston. A little coincidental, didn't you think? That's because it was me, my plane up there shooting at your little toy boat. Didn't you see me? I had the pilot tip the wing to wave at you and everything. Oh right, you wouldn't have seen me because you were too busy on the deck, cowering. Anyway, I thought you could use a break from all that floating and tanning.

Say hi to Boston for me, Morris. Never thought I would miss the dump like I am missing it. I wonder, if I were at Wisconsin-Madison right now, if I'd be missing home as much.

Nah.

you heard from the guys? I heard that Ivan invaded Laos.

I'm worried about Rudi. I haven't heard from him, but that's not shocking. He told me he wouldn't write to me because I would correct his letters. I don't correct, I just offer friendly advice. I hope he's all right. He's still got you watching over him, right?

Try to look up once in a while, too. You might just see me.

And don't forget to watch over Morris, right? Right?

See you soon, pal.
Beck

How did he know I was cowering? Maybe it *was* him up there. The jerk.

I'm more homesick than ever now. I'm going home, will be there in a matter of hours, and I'm almost literally sick to my stomach with homesick. I'll see people, I'll see my mom, I'll eat well and sleep in my own bed and the world will not constantly undulate beneath my feet, and all this is good — no, great — stuff.

But I'll be home to a home that doesn't have Rudi and Beck and Ivan in it. I've never really known a home like that, at least not since I reached the age of really *knowing* things.

So, is that really home?

The most loving and strangulating hug in human history answers my question as soon as I walk through the door.

Of course this is home. I am home.

"Ma, please," I gurgle, the breath squeezed right out of me. She has her head on my chest, her strong arms pythoning my rib cage, and she's quietly crying. I have seen this phenomenon maybe three times in my life, the crying. "Please, Ma, don't," I plead. It is not sloppy sobbing. There are no cries to the heavens of *my son, my son, thank God he's alive*. But in her own way, in *our* way, this is a highly emotional demonstration.

"How is it possible that you got skinnier?" she asks, examining each rib with her fingers the way a tailor would check seams.

"It isn't possible," I say rather feebly, "because I'm not skinnier."

"You're telling me? You are telling *me* about *this*?" She gestures at the totality of me, a sweeping gesture from my head down to my feet as if I am a magic trick she just conjured out of nothing.

She raised me all by herself after we lost my dad. So in a way, I am exactly that.

I'm wearing my uniform, which if you have ever seen the uniform of the United States Navy, you will realize it exaggerates whatever body you've got. Brilliant white flared trousers topped by a brilliant white blouse and a blue kerchief, all topped by the white cupcake hat. If you're fat or short or tall, you're fatter or shorter or taller in this getup. If you're thin . . .

"Get in here," Ma demands, pulling me by the hand through the front hall toward the kitchen. I can smell her meatballs percolating away in her homemade sauce. I can smell that there are forty of them. Just for me. It's ten a.m., and I know this meal has been on for a minimum of four hours.

"I was going to take you out to eat tonight," I say as she just about throws me into my chair. The kitchen set. Aluminum frame. Two-foot by two-foot table with a pebbled silver Formica top. Just-about-padded red vinyl seat and back on the chairs. I want to be buried with this set.

"So who says you can't take me out? Tonight is a whole day away, and you have a good few meals to catch up on."

I spend a good portion of the day eating, and still she doesn't change her mind about going out for dinner. Then the curse of the Navy uniform starts to grab me, and I feel like a loaf of bread stuffed into a half-loaf bag.

"That's more like it," Ma says, standing in front of me, in front of my bedroom door. She pats my stomach with great professional chef satisfaction. I'm not any bigger, just more like a garden hose that got a rat stuck in it.

"Where are we going to eat tonight, Ma?" I ask, and I am so looking forward to this exchange.

"Oh, no place special. I don't want to be any trouble. Someplace nice, inexpensive . . ."

"Anthony's Pier 4," I say powerfully. It feels really good.

She gasps. "Oh, my, no. That is just nonsense. All we need to do is —"

Cheesy as it sounds, I take the greatest delight yet in drawing my wallet out of my pants pocket, opening it up, and fanning a selection of bills I am sure she has not seen since my father died. And quite possibly not before then, either.

She gasps again.

"I thought you were in the Navy, not the Mafia."

"Ma. I get paid. And I don't spend hardly any of it."

She is actually blushing. This is my most successful day as a son, topping my graduation, even. And it may be my peak, so I plan to milk it.

"So, lady," I say, pointing at her, "while I'm taking

my nap, you can just call Anthony's Pier 4 and make us a reservation."

I approach my bed with a grin on my face. Ma always thought of Pier 4 like it was some kind of holy grail of dining experiences, talked about it as if it was this mystical, not-really-possible ideal that was great to think about, without ever quite getting there. Now she's getting there.

I strip off my crisp Navy issue whites and take devilish pleasure in dropping them right there on the floor. It's like escaping the regimented military life and slipping back into my kid self all in one smooth, sloppy move.

I flop onto my bed.

How did this happen?

I stare up straight over my bed. My room is upstairs, where my mother and I occupy the top half of my uncle's two-family house. They don't talk to each other, so it's like we own a house to ourselves but just never use the downstairs part. I'm on the gabled front of the house, and the ceiling has slants and angles all over. On the tilted surface that I would always stare straight into while lying on my back, there is my great big poster of Tony Conigliaro. It's a collage of him batting, playing center field for the Red Sox, and signing autographs for kids at the park. Covering the other sloped wall, just on the opposite side of my one window, is the great up-close shot of Bill Russell leaping, torso-to-torso, to block the shot of the immense Wilt Chamberlain. Behind my head, over the headboard, is Richard Petty and his blue-and-red number 43 winning Daytona.

How did this happen?

How did these posters get so . . . small? How did they lose their zing?

This is my room, my life, my *me*. I am lying on my scuffed-up pine colonial mini poster bed, which feels noticeably smaller than it did the last time I slept in it only seven months ago.

And Tony C. and Russ suddenly look . . . what? Stupid. That cannot be. They're great men. But what they are doing, what looked to me like the most important jobs in the world, now looks like a massive waste of some amazing physiques.

It cannot be. I cannot let it be.

I'm in my underwear, and I pop up out of bed, duck under the baseball poster without looking at it again, and go to my window. I look out at the neighborhood as I know it, at the world as I knew it. I look out over my two modest little swimming trophies from Jamaica Plain Youth Week that stand on my windowsill, raising their tiny arms for attention.

I stare out over the Sem, the Seminary, where I played about fifty thousand innings of baseball. Looking off beyond that is Hyde Square, where I was first ever allowed to go to the store by myself.

The Seminary used to look to me like Yankee Stadium set inside of a great big national park. It's not. It's a Little League park, in the backyard of some school, surrounded by a brick wall. The store, Fargasin's, is so close, my mother could have yelled her order out the window and got it delivered as quick as I could get it.

The USS *Boston* is bigger than Boston, Massachusetts.

I fall back on my bed and close my eyes, figuring after a rest I will adjust again and wake up to the world I knew.

As I fade to sleep, "Anchors Aweigh" starts playing away in my head.

Anchors Aweigh my boys, Anchors Aweigh.
Farewell to college joys, we sail at break of
day-ay-ay-ay . . .

The bell is ringing. It is ringing, hard and incessant and louder than I ever remember it ringing before. I jump up and get down the stairs and out the door where everybody is waiting and screaming at me and we start racing straight down the street toward school. Me, and Ivan, and Rudi, and Beck racing to school and we are late and it is all my fault so everybody is screeching mad at me.

Except for Vera. Vera is running beside me, silent and smiling, as we hurry to school and the screeching is incessant.

And a jet, a MiG-21 fighter, comes curving out of the sky ahead. It angles and heads straight into the path to the school. It drops, slings low, and the screeching of the jet engines and of the guys is fearsome as the jet strafes the bunch of us, shredding us with bullets 'til we all go down, falling over each other, bleeding and coming to pieces, and I can see every eye of every guy in the pile of guys that is us, and they all stare in disgust at me. Except Vera, who seems okay with it all.

I jump up out of bed to the clanging bell. I can actually hear the morning school bell from my bed in the spring and summer when the window is open. More days than I would want to admit, that bell got me out of bed and racing to school because Ma was already two hours at work before I had to be up.

But it's not the school bell now, it's the clanging, dinging trolley making its way down South Huntington Avenue. I have been sleeping for a couple of hours at least. Long enough to have just about worked up my appetite again for dinner.

Although this dinner is hardly about appetite.

I go to my closet and select some nice, fancy Pier 4 clothes. I slip into my royal blue shirt and charcoal gray pants and realize these are the clothes I wore to my graduation and the dinner afterward, and I realize as well that they are looser on me now. It was only to Fontaine's, up the road in Dedham, for boneless fried chicken. But it meant a lot to Ma. She was dressed all the way up to the nines — which is just the way I find her when I step out into the kitchen.

"You look a million, Ma," I say, because she does. It could be Easter Sunday, she looks that good with her pink dress and matching short jacket.

She does not return the compliment.

"What?" I say, palms out, all defensive like I've smashed a window with a baseball. She hasn't said anything, but trouble is obvious.

"What are you wearing?"

I look myself over. "My best?"

She shakes her head. "I have not been chewing my fingernails down all through the news every evening for nothing. The people of Anthony's Pier 4 are going to know that I am having dinner with my hero son who is over there risking his life for *their* prime rib and lobster thermidor. So just reverse course or abandon ship or whatever it is you do, sailor, and go in that room and put on that handsome uniform of yours. That is an order."

Her words do not begin to tell the story of how funny she is. Or how scary.

I'm back in the room and back in the uniform in mere seconds. As I'm tucking, straightening, smoothing, I walk back through the door and notice there is one big bloom of a tomato stain on my left thigh.

If the suit were red, my mother would still notice the red stain.

The suit is, of course, not red.

"Right," she says, twirling away from me in disgust. She stomps down the hall and I scamper after her.

"Ma, Ma."

"Don't talk," she says. "Just forget it. I am calling Mr. Anthony Athenas to cancel our dinner at Anthony's Pier 4 because my son, who is supposed to be saving the world, can't even eat a few meatballs without making a disaster out of his uniform."

She says the name of the restaurant like an incantation, and the name of the owner as if he personally took her reservation, which is unlikely. But she is accomplishing her aim anyway, which is to make me feel like an embarrassing baboon.

"It was not a few meatballs," I say. "It was about a thousand."

"You are defending freedom," she says. "Look at your pants!"

She still has her back to me when I catch up, grabbing her shoulders. They are actually trembling. I turn her around.

Her face is laminated with tears again. And it's worse yet. The lines of her face are not recognizable to me. As if her real face has been glazed with those tears, frozen in a freezer, then cracked with a hammer to create fractures and fissures and all kinds of unwelcome wrong angles.

"Ma?" I say, half laughing, all nervous, "it's a little stain."

"Blood," she says. "Looks like blood. There is an artery" — she makes a slashing gesture across her own inner thigh — "you could die . . . it never stops . . . on the TV . . . it . . . never . . . stops. We all know these things now. . . ."

I grab her and I hold her and she trembles enough that it reminds me of the tremors coming up from under the ship during bombardment, but I don't think I'll share that story. I just keep holding her and I tell her that together we can get this stain out. It's the kind of challenge she loves anyway. She's ready to let go now but I don't let her, because if she sees me crying, then I just don't know what kind of situation we'll have on our hands and we just might end up disappointing Mr. Athenas after all.

I had no idea. How could I be so stupid as to think she wasn't going to be right there with me every bloody step of the way?

When we stroll through the front doors of Anthony's Pier 4, after walking along the Fish Pier, it is everything I always imagined it would be. The only reason I had even imagined it was anything at all was because of Ma's talking about it like it was the restaurant version of a trip to the crying Mary statue at Lourdes. Myself, I was impressed enough with the Fish Pier.

I am finding myself at home with piers and ships, with the smell of the ocean and even sulfuric decaying seaweed.

And I'm wondering how the boys are all doing.

The hostess could not be nicer. She actually salutes me as she seats us. Ma is beaming and gleaming, possibly as proud of her miracle de-staining job on my pants as anything else. Probably not, though.

I am staring at the glory that is Anthony's menu. There is more ocean life on one page here than I have sailed over all these months. I glance up periodically to catch Ma not really looking very closely at her menu.

She is glancing at it but mostly swimming in the surroundings.

I have the clam chowder, she has the shrimp cocktail. She has the poached salmon while I have the broiled scrod, a fish so mythically delicious I doubt it even exists in nature.

But the truth is, I would find it all wonderful because Ma is finding it all so wonderful, which she would do even if they brought her a boiled shoe.

"Everyone is looking at you in your uniform," she says. "Now aren't you glad you wore it?"

"I am, Ma," I say, quite honestly. But I'm glad because of how she's feeling.

"Can I have an Irish coffee?" she asks me, impishly, as we're served Ma's strawberry cheesecake and my key lime pie.

The tide has now, officially, turned.

She is asking *my* permission.

I have never seen my mother so proud, so happy.

Almost too happy.

When the coffee's done, the bill comes, and my head starts spinning all over again. I figure the entire USS *Boston* could be fed for three days for the price of this meal.

"The coffee and dessert were on us," says the waitress as I empty my wallet almost completely.

But she's looking at my mother when she says it.

"I feel like I'm in one of those World War Two musicals," Ma says, very conspicuously looking in all directions, attempting eye contact with any diner or passing staff she can lock onto. She is giddy with Irish coffee and pride, and I know already what movie she is thinking of. She loves musicals, she loves World War II, and she loves to imagine that is what war is.

"On the Town," I say. "With Gene Kelly and Frank Sinatra." It's about three sailors on shore leave in 1944. They're dressed just like I am now. That's the only real thing about it.

"Yes," Ma says, bubbly. "Yes, exactly. And the other one."

"There's another one?"

"Yes," she says. "Yes, yes . . . *Anchors Aweigh.*"

I am looking around at everybody in Anthony's Pier 4 Restaurant now. I am staring, ogling, just like my mother's been doing. Only not as she has been doing. I am really looking at their faces, into their eyes. I am really seeing them, while she is projecting MGM musicals onto their faces.

And what am I seeing, in the reality? Nothing. I see nothing everywhere. Nobody is looking back at me. Nobody notices. Nobody knows.

Nobody cares one little bit what I'm doing in this silly sailor suit.

"What's wrong?" Ma asks.

I am not Frank Sinatra. I am not Gene Kelly. "New York, New York! It's a helluva town!" is not ringing in my ears.

"Anchors Aweigh" is, over and over and over.

"Those movies are so unbelievably stupid, Ma," I say, getting up from the table and waiting for her to do the same.

I might as well have just punched her in the head.

CHAPTER FOURTEEN

Mother Ship

I spend the next three days of my leave apologizing to my mother in any way I know how. I do laundry. I cook. I take long walks through the neighborhood with her, some in my uniform, some in normal civvies. Gradually, I make my way back.

But back where? More with every walk, this does not feel like home. I want to *be* home, without a doubt. But I just can't seem to find it.

The last morning, I stand on Peters Hill, looking out over the city of Boston, ready to head back to the ship of *Boston*. I'm anxious now to go. I never thought I would say that. The people I have met have all been polite, but nobody is giving me any of that "go get 'em" stuff like in the movies.

Instead, they say:

"Just come home safe."

"Keep your head down."

"Don't be a hero."

That last one came from Mrs. Lahar, my sixth grade teacher, who now lives in a retirement home halfway between my house and my old school.

I laughed at first. "Don't be a hero? Mrs. Lahar, you were the one who taught me about heroes. You were the most gung-ho history teacher I ever came across, before or since."

She nodded, then pointed a long finger at me with the same old authority. "There are a lot of causes to die for, Morris. Come home from that pointless and immoral war and find one." Then she kissed me on the cheek. "And try and keep an eye on that idiot friend of yours while you're there."

She was walking away when I tried to pull us both out of it. "You mean Beck, of course," I said.

She stopped, turned, and looked as if I had just torn a scab off her.

"What a waste," she said sadly.

So all I can think of now, as I look at the skyline of my lifelong hometown is, I don't belong here. I don't understand this war — or any war, now that I'm in the middle of one — but I understand I'm supposed to be somewhere and this is not that somewhere right now. If Beck, Ivan, and Rudi are in Southeast Asia, then Southeast Asia is where I belong.

How can that be *pointless and immoral*, to fight for one's friends? It can't be. It can't.

I'm headed back two days earlier than originally planned, because I've been called back. Something is up, and I'm not sorry to go and find out what it is.

Ma, sensing some of what is in me — sensing, of course, all that's in me — is torn to shreds but also not blubbering when I break away from the visit's final hug.

"Do what you need to do," she says. "Get it done, and then come back to me. All of you, just do your jobs and get home."

"Yes, ma'am," I say, and head down the road five pounds heavier. I can at least carry the scent of home, the essence of it, as I go. It is the scent of meatballs, basil, garlic, and spring onions. And of Pond's cold cream, Chanel No. 5, and Alberto V-O 5 hairspray.

I just hope it'll all be the same when I return.

I get a shock when I report.

"Reassigned?" I say, reading the notice on the big board at the naval station at the South Boston Shipyard.

The USS *Boston* is no longer my home. Seems that it's not just the Terrier missiles that are suddenly surplus to requirements.

The notice tells us to report to the mother ship one last time to collect personal belongings, say good-byes, and read the new assignments that have been posted. There is a list of names on this notice, probably ten percent of the ship's crew, who will be moved.

I wonder if it's a coincidence that every one of the guys I bunk with is being transferred. Except, of course, Vera, who transferred himself. I'm thinking it's not a coincidence. Is there such a thing as a suicide virus?

I get to the ship, make my way down to The House. I pass under the 8-inch cannons, detouring for one last sight of the Terrier guided missiles, which the war has left behind but still look ready to come off the bench and get in the game.

All the other guys are already there when I reach sleeping quarters. There's a lot of laughing, head-slapping, shoulder-punching. Hugging, crying, any of that stuff is just not on the menu.

The Navy appears to have reassigned us in twos. Seven is playing his guitar, all packed and sitting in his rack, encouraging Huff to get a move on so they can get to their new assignment on the tank landing ship *Westchester County*. Bruise and Rascal have their bags over their shoulders, itching to report to their new life aboard the destroyer *Sacramento*.

Vera's belongings have been packed up by somebody and are waiting to be collected. Even his dog tags, which he opted not to take with him to the bottom of the sea, sit on top of it all, waiting.

"Where the action is, pal," Moses says, grabbing me in a half-headlock. I'm reading the postings list, trying to make sense of it.

"What is this, 'RAF'?" I ask. Really, I should know. Really, I don't. "Does it mean we've been transferred all the way to the British Royal Air Force?"

"Riverine Assault Force vessel, Mo. It's a floating tank they're putting us on, guns everywhere. We are now part of the Mobile Riverine Force, working together with the sad fools of the Army. We go right upriver, into the very heart of this whole crazed show. We deliver Army jokers way up-country, we go back and forth and supply Army jokers, and when the time comes, we go back up and collect whatever's left of them Army jokers. All the while we blast away at everything that moves."

I just keep staring at the list. "Oh," I say.

Moses points at my designation letters. "At least you finally got your wish, Mr. Communications. You're a radioman."

I brighten up right away. All I ever really wanted was to be in communications, whatever craft they put me on. So not only could I watch over my pals, I might be able to contact them as well. Just to hear them . . .

Another happy thought occurs to me. "So I won't have to do any shooting?"

"Oh, no," Moses says, laughing. "Everybody on that ship is shooting, pal. Even the cook has to be shooting, if you want to get up- and downriver in one piece."

"Oh," I say again. "Oh."

With very little fanfare, I go to my rack and pack up the remains of my life aboard USS *Boston*. It all peters out to the end.

"See ya" and "Good luck" and "Maybe we'll catch up again" are about all we give to each other, all we get from each other. Just like that, The House empties for the last time.

"Come on," Moses says, "let's go. I don't want to spend one more minute than necessary on the USS *Crackerbox*."

I would have thought Moses had been the happiest guy on the whole ship.

But maybe I don't know anything.

We're headed out the door when we bump right into the big Marine officer coming in. Moses and I snap right to attention, salute, and stand aside as the officer walks past.

Col. Rivera it says on his name tag.

We stand frozen in place as he walks silently to Vera's rack.

He stands over the rack, over the really puny little hump of belongings that are what is left of his son. He stands, hunched over it, exactly the way a person pauses on his way past a coffin at a funeral.

He does not move for the longest time. It is so tense, so sad, so gut-wrenching, I would throw my own self into the ocean right now if I had half a chance.

Colonel Rivera breaks the stillness by saluting his son.

I am certain it is the first and only time he has done so. I am wondering how things might have been different if he had done it, just once, while Vera was alive.

"You men can go," the colonel says, his voice cracking but still clearly the authority in the room. "Move on, gentlemen. Please, move on."

We don't need to be told again. We scramble as Colonel Rivera sits on the rack, his back still to us, gathering up the dog tags, picking up — and smelling close and deep — his boy's shirt.

He is definitely humming softly as Moses and I depart.

Anchors Aweigh.

CHAPTER FIFTEEN

Blue Water No More

After reporting, with our lives stuffed into these long canvas duffel bags, we are once more transported across the ocean, on a converted World War II troop ship, back to the action. Only this time, we're taken much deeper into the action.

For only the second time in about a hundred years, the US Navy has divided itself in two. My life on the USS *Boston*, floating off the coast and on the ocean, was part of the Blue Water Navy. What a lot of people would call *the easy war*.

From now on, that won't be the case at all. I am now part of the Brown Water Navy, where life is a whole lot more complicated.

Because of the geography of Vietnam, it eventually became obvious to the people who decide such things that if we wanted to make progress there had to be a more clever approach than *one if by land, two if by sea*. There is certainly a great deal of land around here, and it sure is blessed with a good long coastline. But there's much more of what you might refer to as *other* terrain for fighting.

There is a lot of jungle in Vietnam. There is a *lot* of jungle. And it is cut up, north-south, east-west, and every possible combination of all that, with rivers. Thousands of miles of rivers. If you are going to move effectively around here, if you are going to find the enemy, engage the enemy, deliver troops, equip them, move them from place to place, and above all cover them with the Navy's special brand of protection, you are simply going to have to use a good bit of boat power to do it.

And where that jungle and those waterways come right up close and personal to each other? Well, that is about the most dangerous place on planet Earth.

Welcome to my new home. Welcome to the Mekong Delta.

They are called river monitors, because of their resemblance to the *Monitor*, one of the first two armored warships, from the Civil War. I studied that bit, the *Merrimac* and the *Monitor*, bouncing cannonballs off each other like it was nothing more than a game of dodgeball.

One look at my new place of work, and I know things are going to get a lot more interesting than that.

There will be only eleven of us on board, which means much more responsibility, and much more risk.

Moses was right: This is a floating tank we are looking at as we stand waiting on the barge to be welcomed aboard. But what even Moses didn't realize was this is also a beast. A growling, snarling, howling, grinning, booming, fire-breathing sea monster.

It's known as the battleship of the river force because it's designed to provide heavy-duty support to our Army brothers in the thickest of battles along the banks and some ways inland. We're so armored, and so armed, it looks like movement was just an afterthought for the craft. This creature looks to me as if it could defeat any and all comers up and down the river all by itself. The forward turret has a 40-mm cannon and an M-60 machine gun. Halfway up ship, dug in as if they were in foxholes on land, are an 81-mm mortar and two .50-caliber machine guns. The rear carries two 20-mm cannons, another two .50-caliber machine guns, and four more M-60 machine guns.

Mounted up front and center at the nose of the operation are two smaller turrets, each with one more machine gun mounted side by side with . . .

"Moses," I ask, having not seen these bits of kit before, "what is that?"

Moses can barely speak. "We're on a Zippo, man. I didn't know we were gonna be on a Zippo!"

"A Zippo?"

He turns to me and grabs me by the shoulders in an almost teary embrace. "Zippo. Like the lighter. Those ain't cannons, Mo. Those are flamethrowers."

We both turn in silence back to the hugeness we've been assigned to. Like Moses, I am now entranced, looking again over every inch of this ugly, mighty *thing* floating here under the ungodly Vietnamese sun. It ain't pretty, that's for certain. It's got tires strapped here and there as bumpers, it's got steel caging around the turrets, sandbags packed within the caging. The turrets themselves look like they were copied straight out of some medieval book of castles and pounded out of metal — and then, while they were at it, they roped in an honest-to-goodness dragon for laughs. It's got crazy eyes and teeth painted straight across the bow, and somebody has printed *Burning Sensation* across the side.

The river monitor could easily have been the brainchild of an inspired twelve-year-old death merchant with a sense of fun. Male, naturally.

I look to Moses, who just keeps running his eyes up and down and all over the vessel admiringly.

"What do you make of this?" I finally ask him.

"My boy, I am stone-cold in love."

The communications shelter is the spot on the boat where I do my most professional work. *Shelter* isn't quite the right word, since the area where I do most of my communicating is lodged pretty plainly on deck, in between the forward turret and the midship turret, which looms over everything. I'm surrounded by the same bar armor as most of the other stations, though it's hard to see how that really protects us from, say, bullets. For most of the time, like now, when it is life threateningly sunny, we also have this canvas sunshade rigged up over my head that makes my station kind of like a patio, sociable and all, but still not much protection from rocket-propelled projectiles.

The water is just as advertised. The opposite of what I knew in the Blue Water Navy, this soup is a couple of shades darker than the sunset, a thin, murky, scary mystery.

There is something honest about that.

The captain has trained me up in the fairly simple business of communications, and has given me the even more important information about who among the vast population of Army personnel we will be communicating with. I take regular updates from the command center in Saigon, letting us know what parts of the river we need to be patrolling and what we are to look out for. And if we see anything that looks out of the ordinary in a hey-that-could-kill-us kind of way, I need to be contacting the center for the green light on doing something about it. Other times we are loading up supplies for the Army grunts, or cleaning and oiling and generally babying our implements of destruction as if our lives depended on it.

"Our brothers in arms throughout this whole great endeavor of the Riverine Assault project are the Ninth Division."

"Huh," I say. "I have an old pal in the Ninth."

"Second Brigade . . ."

"Wow. That's . . ."

"Thirty-fourth Artillery."

It's one hundred and seven degrees in the shade, and I get a chill.

"Ivan," I say right out loud.

"Yeah," the captain says, "they're pretty much all called Ivan. Or Bruno, or Knuckles, or somethin'. Listen, I'll just leave you to it, then."

He leaves me to it. This is the beauty of my job, if there is beauty to it. The *it* he is leaving me to is working on the task of radioing my pal Ivan. The communications job on one of these dinky tubs is nothing like it would have been on one of the monster ships. Those things have every which kind of radar, sonar, electronic gear for getting and giving information. By contrast, what I have here can look more like a glorified telephone operator's gig. Sometimes not even much glorified. But it does mean I am the man, in charge of the box. And in my downtime I have just this little bitty bit of authority, all my own.

It would be so great to hear his actual voice. To hear any of the guys' voices.

Maybe I will get better at this, but I seem to be chasing my tail in my effort to reach Ivan. I suppose it is fair to expect the infantry to be on the move and fighting as long as they are here, but still, I figure, he could take one lousy call.

I laugh when I hear myself think that. I will talk to him eventually. We have jobs to do, and just like I was hoping, I am one step — actually several steps — closer to what I thought of as my mission when I first joined up. I am watching over my boys. Providing backup and cover while they are out there doing the truly hard and dangerous dirty work of this war. And I have the added bonus of being The Communicator, pulling us all together. Which is really as it should be.

We're cruising south down the Mekong, returning from dropping a load of Army troops off about halfway to the Cambodian border. Cruising back down should be the simple part, but nothing is simple in this brown water. We can go days without seeing anything hostile on the banks, but that by no means indicates that hostility isn't hiding in there. Facing the Vietcong sprinkled throughout the heavy foliage of the southern riverways or in the hills beyond is a much more dicey and uncertain thing than taking on the regular army of the North.

Ping!

It starts with just one shot bouncing off of plate metal. Then two and three and six, like popcorn starting up.

"Incoming! Incoming! Incoming!" somebody bellows, just a little after we have all figured that something's incoming. Bullets are zinging past, whistling right by my ears, dinging off all the various angles of metal all over the boat. Unlike the *Boston*, nobody has to sound any sirens when the action kicks off down here. You know, and you move.

And you realize that you are close to death, for crying out loud, or death is close to you, and will be from now until you get discharged.

I scramble to my battle station, which is high up in the midship turret. I feel like a carnival clown, so exposed, so ready for plucking. Guys are shouting; the sun, finally setting, is making the horizon glow a beautiful brown. We can't see the bullets as they sail for every one of us.

Even though it's a tiny fraction of the size of the giant cruiser of my first tour, the monitor feels as if it has every bit as much firepower. Every time the gunner beside me fires his cannons, it sounds and feels as if a plane has crashed into something right beside me.

I must be doing my staring and cringing routine, which I perfected out at sea and which will *not* be tolerated here, because the gunner, Everett, hollers at me, "Use that thing, right now!"

I have a field telephone slung like a knapsack over my shoulder, but he doesn't mean that. With a crew of eleven, everyone has multiple jobs, and everyone knows if you fail to do yours.

I settle in at my second duty.

I am a man of war now, for real. Settled in alongside Everett, I take my place behind my .50-caliber machine gun. I pepper every bit of coast I see, where tracer bullets lace through the evening air like murderous mosquitoes trying to put us away.

I won't lie. It feels good. I have my helmet on, and as I blast away, the shaking of the gun, the boat, my bones, keeps jiggering the helmet down over my eyes. I push it back every time without missing a beat, and I fire-fire-fire like it's my sworn nemesis out there who has insulted my mother and killed all my pals and sworn to knife every man, woman, and child I've ever known.

The thing, finally, that makes shooting at a person feel right? It's shooting at them. Shooting a gun is the thing that convinces you of the rightness of shooting.

Because it works. It solves problems, after all, right? I can feel it right this second, as the repeating action of the machine gun shakes my hands to a state of absolute numbness that works its way from my fingers up my hands and all into me everywhere. I am not, for the moment, afraid. I am not useless or out of place or just getting by. I am shooting something, stopping something — I am meeting aggression with aggression, saving my friends in the process, saving everybody's friends in the process.

As my bullets penetrate the jungle, I swear I can actually feel my fears and worries and problems go down. I am *forcing* them down with my .50-caliber machine gun.

The mortar fire booms from below us, pushing the massive bulk of the monitor down farther into the water. We hear as the shots connect with their target in the distance. The explosion is unbelievable, as if it's an explosion of explosions, two rockets hitting each other nose-to-nose in midair.

BOOM goes Everett's cannon again, and a whole section of jungle seems to buckle under the blast fifty yards beyond the bank. My instruction is to hammer away at whatever tracers I see coming out of the bush, and I have to say I'm adapting to it. Part of me would rather be on the line to our big buddies, calling in coordinates for the helicopter gunships, the killer Seawolves, to come in and finish them off.

But sometimes it's your own fight.

I don't know how we're doing it, but we're firing on all cylinders, with machine guns, howitzers, mortar fire, and rockets obliterating whatever threat has just been unleashed on us. Gradually, over maybe twenty minutes of heat and holler, we put the attack out entirely.

There's one last, loud salvo from shore, then Everett throws an arm around my neck as the captain powers up the monitor to head upstream. The air is filled with sulfur, smoke, and sunset. Everything around us is burning.

The brown water is like gravy, bubbling in our wake. To make us more nimble on shallow water, we have light, crisp armor plating and jets instead of propellers pushing us on.

My heart has never pounded like this. I take a moment to watch all thirty-two inches of my sweaty chest puff crazy like a hummingbird. Then I look back out at the water, the banks, the low sky ceiling. There is something beautiful there, in the smoking murky scene we're fleeing.

"Wow," I say to Everett. "Who did we shoot?"

"Who knows?" He laughs weakly. "We got 'em all, though, whoever they were."

There's something wrong. I look down at where Everett's arm is draped over and down my chest. There's blood. His blood.

"You're hurt," I say.

He tries to wave it off, but he can't. He's leaning hard on me now.

"It's just my arm," he says. Then he collapses and pulls me to the deck with him.

After two other guys take Everett off me and lay him down, I radio ahead and make sure medical coverage is waiting. Part of the special nature of the Riverine Force is that all its parts seem to be in motion at once. There are medical teams stationed on various boats. Some craft are dedicated medical units, like great big amphibious ambulances. And there are units positioned all up and down the river from the Delta to the DMZ, harboring small but expansive med teams that can do everything from lancing a boil to relieving you of a gangrene-filled hand before it's too late. We are directed to a spot about six klicks from where we are, where one of the stationary pontoons has just the stuff to make Everett right again.

"I don't need any help," Everett insists, despite not

being able to get himself off that very bit of deck he landed on. "It'd take more than this to get me to go to no stupid doctor. I'm made of tougher stuff than that. What do I look like, Blue Water Navy or something?"

"Hah," Moses says, standing over us. "He got ya there, Mo."

"Everett," the captain says, "everybody appreciates your toughness, but this cannot stay on this boat."

Cap takes Everett's hand and raises his arm to show Everett the extent of his own wound.

The arm hangs there like something in a butcher's window. Everett's been hit by who-knows, but whatever it was took a chunk the size of my fist out of the underside of his biceps. It is seeping blood and fibrous tissue, like a wolf bite has torn the arm nearly in half.

Everett's remaining toughness spills onto the deck, his eyes rolling back in his head. Moses cradles him to the deck while I tie a fast and tight tourniquet around the highest part of his arm I can get a purchase on. The bandage is already soaked through by the time I get it tied, but it's at least making a temporary barrier to prevent his heart pumping all his blood out into the war.

Another crewman comes running with the med bag. Cap grabs it from him, tears it open, and shoots a vial of morphine straight into Everett's arm, then another shot, of antibiotics, the needle driving right into the pulp of the open shoulder muscle.

"He's gonna lose that arm, Cap," Moses says, perching exactly between question and statement.

"He loses any more blood, the arm won't be an issue," Cap says, looking off to where we need to take the patient.

He's not dead when we leave him, so that's good. By the time we've removed him to the floating med station, though, it looks like we've all been shot. Moses, myself, and Cap all get a quick appraisal from the field doctors trying to satisfy themselves that the whole crew hasn't been shot up. We are eventually allowed to leave Everett and take ourselves back out.

I am looking myself up and down as we move along the river again. Looking at the blood on my arms, my thighs, all over the front of my shirt. When I was a kid, I had to turn away whenever I got cut, to keep myself from getting woozy. Now it's lots of blood, and I cannot stop staring at it, fascinated. I sniff at it, trying to get a scent. Some completely demented urge, but powerful just the same, comes over me to taste it.

"Wash that business off yourself," snaps Cap, already cleaned up and re-shirted. I guess I've been fascinated by Everett's blood for longer than I realized.

I guess somebody else's blood is an altogether different thing.

There is a rotation when somebody leaves ship like Everett does. A full compliment has eleven enlisted men and the captain. Guys choose jobs according to length of time on board this particular boat, and Everett's job was one of the lower ones, with him being perched in the highest spot of all the battle stations. He liked it, though, for the view, for being able to survey all before him, as he put it, and I could certainly appreciate his logic.

I wouldn't appreciate having his job, though.

He's going to live, but there's no guarantee he's going to be back with this crew anytime soon. He isn't being replaced by anyone right off, so I find Moses up in the tall turret beside me as we go on another evening up and down through the syrupy Mekong River. Central Command says a few of the slower troop carriers have been pestered by pods of nasties dug into the banks making night raids, and we have been politely asked to flush them out and start a proper fight.

"It's far too quiet along this river at night," Moses says as we lean over the bar armor, scanning for anything indigenous and deadly along the banks. He is right beside me now, but when it kicks off, his battle station, the cannon, sits more or less just up over the shoulder of machine gunner me. He's at the big gun up high above everything, watching over it all. It occurs to me that this is just the situation I envisioned would be best, right after he beat me senseless on the *Boston*. Comforting.

"I am sweltering," I say.

"You're always sweltering, man."

"Come on, Moses, you have to feel the difference. It's like breathing through sponges."

"Yeah, it is a little more moist than usual."

The sky doesn't have any of the range of colors we usually get during these early evening runs. There's a gray-brown sameness to almost everything, the river and sky pressing together to sandwich us out of air entirely.

I sit down on the small balcony of the mid-turret deck and take out the phone for another try. I go through the connection protocol for Ninth Division, Second Brigade, Thirty-fourth Artillery.

"Man, why don't you just be cool and wait for a call. You seem far too anxious. Gotta play hard to get."

"Listen," I say, "he's the only one I haven't heard from. Of my three pals, right? The other two guys, at least they sent me letters. . . ."

He does what he thinks is an imitation of my voice,

as if I were a seventy-year-old lady. "You never call me . . . you never write . . ."

"I'm serious, Moses. It just seems even worse knowing that Ivan is right here, part of this very op. Ninth Division, Second Brigade, Thirty-fourth Artillery . . . and I can't even get a call through to him."

I look to the rear to see the aft gunners have cast fishing lines. This is about as calm as things get here.

I felt a lot less nervous when we were all just shooting.

"Maybe it's you," Moses says. "Maybe you aren't the great communicator after all. You should probably just give that job up, man, and follow your true calling."

"Which is?"

"I saw you shooting, friend. Machine-Gun Mo should be your name. You were lovin' it."

I shake my head. I feel my helmet wobble around. "Just doing my job. It helps me to think of my people out there. It helps to make sense of shooting people I don't even know. . . . My brother's enemy is my enemy, right?"

Moses takes a long, slow suck on the saturated air. He looks off in the other direction from me, upriver.

"That's swell, Mo, it really is. Provided you know who your brother is."

I swivel my head around, smiling at him, adjusting my helmet again, checking him out. He's not smiling.

"You don't know?" I ask.

"Why do you think I'm up here at the very peak of harm's way?"

I shrug. "I thought you were ordered up here."

He pauses again. "I was. But I would've volunteered anyway. Experience tells me I don't want nobody behind me with a gun."

I try again. "Camaraderie? Allies?"

Now he smiles. "Mo, I have met some Vietnamese people who I wouldn't mind having a beer with. I have also met some Australian sailors who I would gladly shoot if the Navy would let me."

This is making me sad. This is a situation I have not pondered. Some part of me swallowed that whole brothers-in-arms ideal that they started feeding us on the first day of basic, and I feel a little bit like a stupid kid to be finding out it was maybe a fairy tale.

"So you don't trust anybody?" I ask.

He looks disappointed in me now. As if, while he was damaging my idealism, I was spoiling his cynicism, and neither one of us is happy with the outcome.

"Okay, I trust *you*. Happy now?"

Do I make myself a sap forever now if I say yes, in fact, I am, thank you very much, Moses?

It's not the biggest risk I've taken this year.

"Yes, in fact, I am, thank you very much, Moses."

He tries to be stern, I try to be perky. My helmet tips once more over my eyes and Moses laughs.

"Your head isn't even big enough to make that helmet sit up, man," he says, as if that proves how unqualified I am for everything.

One of the two fishermen pulls in something substantial and there's some quiet excitement at the back of the boat. From my perch it looks like some golden-green slimy species I've never seen, but in size and feistiness it closely resembles the really big bluefish that would run in abundance off the coast of Massachusetts in August. That kind of fish is so delicious, I'm welling up with saliva at the thought. Beck and I, too young to know any better, used to refuse to eat when our dads brought them home, a war and a world and a warp away from here.

The fisherman, Foley, holds his rod way up while the fish fights to get free. He swings it around just far enough that the other guy, Marchand, gets a good close-up.

Marchand, sitting behind the machine gun that sits beside the flamethrower, waits just long enough, leans sideways, then *whooosheshoosh* — with a spray that lasts all of an eighth of a second, he fires the flamethrower, and flame broils that fish into something Godzilla wouldn't pick his teeth with.

The smell is acrid, sharp, right past my sinuses and directly up into my brain, even from this distance. The heat, even off that little blast, even in the middle of the heat we already have, is stunning.

The flaming fish drops off the line and back where he came from, unrecognizable to his best friends.

"Jeez," I say, rolling onto my back away from it.

I'm looking right up into Moses's satisfied smile. He's pointing at the flamethrower.

"That's what I want a crack at," he says.

"What's in that stuff?"

"Napalm, baby. Basically, it's highly flammable fuel blended with chemicals that make it thicker, like a gel. So you can shoot it straighter. And it sticks a lot better to the lucky recipients."

"Flaming syrup," I say.

"Close. More like Vaseline Gasoline."

Moses makes his hungry noise.

I look up and all around. The air is definitely changing. It's moving. One way, then back again, then down like an elevator gone crazy.

"There's a storm coming," Cap calls from his spot up front.

I scramble down to the communications shelter, which everybody now just calls The Patio. I try hard to locate Ivan.

These mad storms always make it even harder.

CHAPTER SIXTEEN

Saps and Sappers

It turns out we carry eleven hundred gallons of the stuff on board.

It turns out when they tell you a storm is coming in Vietnam, a *storm* is coming.

It turns out my man Ivan is stationed on a self-propelled barracks ship called *Benewah* that I have probably passed by eighty different times on my way up- or downriver. When I finally do track him through channels upon channels, I find that I could almost have reached him easier by standing on top of the main turret and shouting his name.

Which I can't do now because we're in the company of the lovely Typhoon Elaine.

"Ivan!" I scream into the radio phone while we try desperately to get ourselves docked and back into quarters before the worst of it hits. "Ivan, Ivan, Ivan, man, is it really you?"

"No," he says very quietly for the conversation's

requirements. "I just left a minute ago. Of course it's me, man. Jeez, it's good to hear you."

"It's great to hear you," I shout over the thunder, the wind, and the rain that's like some god of water picking up the ocean and dumping it over us over and over again. Just the general maritime, wartime mayhem, only spiced with my first-ever typhoon. "That is, it would be great to hear you, if I could hear you. You have to shout, Ivan."

"I don't wanna shout. Sorry."

"What are you talking about? You love to shout. You shout over nothing. You shout when the Patriots don't protect the quarterback — which is *every* play. You shout at the movies when the action slows down too much. You shout at hamburgers if they don't have mustard on them. Ivan, pal, it's been months. If you don't shout at me right now, I swear I'm gonna smack ya down."

He doesn't shout. But he does laugh such a real and crystal laugh, it actually clears the phone connection.

"What's so funny?" I say, though I couldn't possibly care as long as he keeps it up.

"The thought of you getting tough with me." He lets the laugh taper off, and a little silence roll in.

Thunder wallops. Lightning strikes probably less than a klick away.

"How are ya, Morris?" he asks.

"They call me Mo here," I say.

He laughs even harder.

"I won't be calling you Mo."

"I wouldn't be letting you."

I have to wait again. "I tried to get tough again there, didn't I?" I say.

"Yeah," he replies through storm crackle and cackle. "And keep it coming. Laughs are a valuable commodity, Morris."

"They are, pal. We can't be long, but I'm dying to hear how you're doing. Why haven't you been writing to me?"

There's another pause.

"You know I don't like to write."

"No, Ivan, I don't know that. Anyway, even Rudi wrote to me a couple of times."

"He wrote to me, too."

"Great. Excellent. How was that?"

"Great," he snaps. "Beck, too."

"Beck, he's probably writing from an office in the Pentagon, pretending he's over here."

"Probably," Ivan says.

The line cracks and kicks, out, then back again.

"We have to cut this short," I say, "but now that we're neighbors, we're going to see how to get together somewhere for an hour someplace. Maybe have a steak."

"Army doesn't have much steak," he says.

"Navy has all the steak," I laugh.

"No wonder everybody hates you."

"That's probably it."

More cracks, more lightning. Cap is shouting for all hands as we near the docking.

"I have to go, Ivan. I'll get back to you. I'll see you. I really want to see you. You okay? I mean of course you're okay. You okay?"

"Yeah," Ivan says in an un-Ivan, unemotional tone that's new to me. "I kill people, man. I'm pretty good at it."

The line hangs up for us. I stare for a second until Cap calls again, and I run up out of my communications shelter that really isn't a shelter at all, into the storm.

Elaine turns out to be a storm like nothing I've seen in my life. I thought the biggest meteorological event a guy could experience would be the big nor'easter snowstorms that hit New England in winter, but I'd do a week of those before I'd endure one of these things again. The volume of rain and the ferocity of the wind are the kind of things you might see in Boston once in your life, but if you did, you would see it for about fifteen minutes. A typhoon blows in and hangs around like the most disgusting uninvited houseguest ever.

At the end of our patrols, crews like us stay on great sea floats moored at stations up and down the Mekong. They started appearing when the Navy decided we were better off being self-sufficient and untouchable, rather than having to do any extra back-and-forthing inland for stuff. Whole floating towns materialized, and ours is this long T-shaped solid dock with seven great barges attached that serve as everything from sleeping quarters to mess hall to supply depot. At any one time they can have a whole flotilla of craft moored up, from a tanker to swift boats and Coast Guard cutters to troop transports or little minesweeping drones that look like heavily armored kayaks.

When Elaine sweeps in to kick our butts, all these craft are there, and more.

She wreaks havoc. We lose power. A security tower crashes right down into the river. The whole entire top tears right off our mess hall. Boats pull loose and travel on their own for miles downriver. Some of the smaller ones flip right up onto land.

And all the while the rain falls like something out of the Bible. I see guys standing in the river, keeping drier in the silt than out of it.

The only thing even somewhat preventing this from being hell is that for three days Elaine is the only thing we're fighting. And while she is the tougher fight, and we actually lose badly, at first there's a place deep inside me that enjoys losing this fight more than winning the other one.

By the third day, though, I feel different. When we're collecting, cleaning, and repairing rather than fighting any foe at all, I very suddenly want to shoot again.

We're on a recovery trip, like we've made dozens of times already. We're towing a stray PBR, which stands for Patrol Boat, River. These boats are the speed and the sense of all the ops here in the Mekong, and while there are scores of new and improvised task craft here all the time, these are the guys we see every time out, spearheading everything.

The PBR's four-man crew are all sitting like holiday pleasure boaters on the front lip of the boat as we tow them up at their much slower than usual pace. The storm left the boat unworkable, which will only last until we get them back to the maintenance float and they will be scouring the river at high speed once —

Pu-boooooom . . .

That is one explosion. I turn quickly toward the PBR from my perch.

Pu-boooooom . . .

The first explosion is bad, leaving only three crew members — or parts of them — stuck clinging to the front rail. One guy hangs on with his one arm, the other one liquidated. Two guys flop on the deck.

The second explosion finishes the work, taking these remains of sailors and belting them from the opposite side.

It reminds me a little of the nature program where the orca whales take the seals and throw them back and forth for fun before finishing off the poor bloody blobs. One blast knocks them one way, then the other back again, the second one creating an absolute fountain of heads and legs and cross sections of torsos, loads of foamy blood topping off the massive column of brown water.

In twenty seconds, it's almost as if they were never there.

It takes me less than thirty more to convince myself that they never were.

Bad dreams are bad, but they are only dreams.

Debris floats in the water while the crew of my boat stares, uniformly numb. Debris. But there's always debris in the Mekong River.

The whole time, we weren't fighting Typhoon Elaine. The whole time, the war wasn't suspended. While we were playing River Rat Boy Scout games, their swimmers, sappers, were operating as usual. Tying off mines along the riverbed, attaching limpet mines to boat hulls like big evil barnacles that would explode once the swimmers were safely away.

The whole time, it was business as usual underneath the river. Of course, they know their land and water and storm better than we do.

I feel the need to talk to my friends.

I feel the need to shoot somebody.

But in what order?

Not that that's a choice for me. The need for revenge is strong, and every fighting man in the service suffers from these sneak attacks, these clever bombs and daring sabotage raids, and every one of us makes noise about teaching the sneaky cowards a good and proper lesson. Lemme at 'em.

Then we inhale, and exhale, and slip into the water to do the only thing we can do. We collect the men, the bits and pieces of them. We tell them we are sorry, we tell them we will do everything humanly possible. And we tell ourselves we know that isn't very much.

All this firepower, and vulnerable as infants.

CHAPTER SEVENTEEN

Vaseline Gasoline

It makes too much sense. Eventually, my grand design would melt all over itself. Operation Overlord, where I'm looking out for my friends from my place of vision and vigilance, is a great idea. If only I were capable.

The more natural outcome would have the brilliant Beck looking out for all of us. And more and more that seems to be what we have.

Hey Pal,

Remember how I took care of you when you were on the USS <u>Boston</u>, getting you bombed and sent home to the real Boston for a vacation? Well, I'm at it again. Sometimes it seems to me like I am over here expressly for the purpose of watching over your shoulder, looking for anything I can do to make your life a little more pleasant or less dangerous.

Guess what they're having me do now. Pruning. Weeding. Making the banks of the Mekong a more Morris-friendly place to play.

Seriously. I am spraying defoliant. Operation Ranch Hand, they call it. I am spraying this wicked concoction called Agent Orange that basically burns the crap out of all the green life growing all around the rivers, up through most of Vietnam and Laos. We kill their crops to make them weak, and we kill their cover so we can get a clear shot at them.

Morris, I've seen it. I've seen the before and the after. It looks like a forest fire has swept through the banks of rivers for three hundred yards either side. Then you hit the Cambodian border, and it's as if someone opened a door from the death planet into the Amazon forest.

You're welcome.

Don't get killed, Morris. Don't waste all my fine work.

Have you heard from Ivan? I haven't. Not one word since basic training, when he told me he was going infantry instead of cavalry because he wanted that "human touch." My guess is he's giving them a lot of touch, but very little humanity.

I don't like the silence, though. If he weren't Ivan, I'd be worried. I saw a local on a sampan the other day stick a fish with a spear. Reminded me of a bluefish. I'd love a piece of blue right now.

Can you talk to Rudi? See if you can radio him, will you? He says he's doing great. He writes once in a while now. Looks like he's writing with a crayon stuck up his nose while he eats at the same time. But at least he writes. He sounds confident. Yeah, I know.

Guys here never talk about winning and losing and all that. They talk about accumulated time, sorties and landings, tonnage, time, time, time.

What are your days like now? A lot hotter than Boston, or Boston, am I right?

Try to talk to Rudi.

Your Man in the Sky

Mail reading time isn't anywhere near as organized an event as it was on the *Boston*. Partly, I guess, because of the more disjointed nature of life down here in the delta. Every layer of existence is wilder and more chaotic than it was when we were cruising at a stately pace way out there on the coast. We have big mother helicopters swooping low all the time, landing every-where, beating the bushes for the enemy, dropping supplies, picking strays up out of the water. Lots of these smaller river craft have their own makeshift heli-pads tacked right onto the boats, a sturdy and fixed version of my canvas sun shield. We come off the boat like a factory ship, we work with hundreds of other boats, thousands of other guys. We work with all the other services.

Life here is less majestic than on the big gliding cruiser I was on in a past life. It's faster, less intimate, less like a neighborhood, more like a freeway. If you have one of those helicopter pads on your roof, an approaching rotor could mean anything when it lands.

Ivan's home, the *Benewah*, has one of those pads.

I've neither seen nor heard from Ivan since the typhoon. He's out there. I'm following along as best I can, tracing the Thirty-fourth Artillery movements as best I can. They're still at it, but he's not turning up on any lists, so he's no casualty.

Like Beck said, though, you'd worry if he wasn't Ivan. Right?

Meanwhile, you don't need a reason to worry about Rudi. I get another letter from him.

Morris Man,

So you did it. You finally joined the action. This is great. Now I don't have to do all the fighting for the two of us anymore. Laugh. I'm just kidding. Actually, I'm fighting for about fifty of us. No fooling, Morris. I have to tell you something, and I want you to believe me.

I am not leaving the Marines when this is over.

I belong here. How many times you figure a guy hears his name called in his whole lifetime? I don't know, either, but ask Beck, 'cause he will probably know the number and then you will have the number of times I hear my name shouted out every single day.

Half of it is for the wrong things.

You know what that means?

Exactly right. Half the time men are screaming my name out here AND IT IS ALL FOR THE RIGHT THINGS! I mean it, man. And even when I don't hear the right kind of screaming, I go and do something screwy on purpose, just to hear my name being screamed.

Morris, I am getting an addiction to screaming. Laugh.

I make whole villages scream and they don't even know who I am.

I am going to tell you another something. Okay? I killed a man. Charlie, VC, right? I killed Charlie. Nothing special, since I kill guys all the time now. But this is a story. I shoot 'em, and I grenade 'em and all that. But this one, we were patrolling and he surprised me because, jee?, these guys — they are like cats and you step right on them in that jungle before you know they are there. I did, too. I really, truly stepped on him.

Hah. Back home what if I stepped on somebody, like I did lots of times? People call me names, smack me in the head, pee on my lunch, right?

But here my actions make sense. I step on him, he jumps right up, I turn and don't let him raise his weapon. Morris, I stabbed him. With my bayonet, right below the belt. I was scared, but I was all energy, too, yeah, so I stick that bayonet in there, and I work it on him like I'm using a great big bread knife on some day-old crusty scali bread. You remember that scali bread, Morris, we used to get day old from Boschetto's? It was so good, but man it was tough cutting.

Right, I cut and I cut until he falls back, falls off my knife, and lands on his seat. He sits a few tics, his hands holding his stomach like he can hold it all in when it's already almost all out. He looks up at me, kind of like crying, but I can't really read these guys' faces, Morris, and he is staring up and I am staring down.

And then the shouting starts. My other guys, the three excellent guys on my patrol, they catch up, standing behind me, and they start chanting my name like whisper-chanting it so as not to attract attention. Ruu-Dee, Ruu-Dee, Ruu-Dee.

So I do what you do. I don't think. (You know I'm good at that.)

I do the whole thing again. Only to his throat.

With the guys chanting "Rudi, Rudi," I stick Charlie just under one ear. I start sawing and I have to even angle to keep him upright but I do it and I mean to stop at his Adam's apple but the chanting doesn't stop so I doesn't stop.

I cut off almost his whole head. I did that. Me.

I never could have done that back home, that's for sure.

The guys went to continue patrol, but I told them I would catch up. I sat down next to

CHARLIE. I just felt like I needed to sit right next to him for a little bit. So I did.

I told him I was sorry. And I thanked him.

How are you doing?

Once you stop being afraid, everything will be okay. Trust me.

Your pal,
Rudi

"You sharing?" Moses says, curling cross-legged on the floor of my communications patio. If I have a friend here and now, it's Moses. I get along with everybody, but there's getting along, and there's Moses, and that's about all I can manage. We have a language of approach when one of us is reading mail. The sweetness-and-light letters and packages are the ones you want to share, so you can see your happiness in the other guy's face. The difficult stuff — the stuff that is too complicated, sad, infuriating — when a guy reads that, he almost always takes on the glazed, mummified look.

"Sharing or staring?" becomes the question.

When I remain silently looking at Rudi's letter, the question kind of answers itself.

Really, he just wanted to share anyway.

Moses shoves a photo in my face. There is a pair of

hands holding up a baby too tiny to hold its own head up. The baby is wearing a tiny T-shirt, which looks like a dress and has print down the front reading SOME-BODY IN VIETNAM LOVES ME.

I'm staring again, but now it's a whole different thing.

I look over, and his eyes are so filled with water, he looks like he might have glaucoma.

"You're a father, Moses?" I say.

"Apparently so."

I actually giggle, feeling something so nice, even one degree removed.

"Well, go ahead and cry, stupid," I say.

"I will not," he says, all butch and ridiculous. "And if you call me *stupid* again, I'm gonna napalm you worse than that fish."

Before he can do that, we get a call on the radio and I take it. We are to haul it as fast as we can, because there is the mother of all firefights and there is blood, US Army blood, Navy blood, spilling and filling this very river. We've been headed to base, but command says to reverse upriver and full-speed it to the fight.

Full speed for this craft is unfortunately not more than six knots, but we give it our all to cover the six-kilometer distance.

It's all happening in a kind of slow motion. Every-body gets to battle stations as soon as I let out the shout.

Captain snags the radio from me and starts banging back and forth with command.

Guys are flying all over the boat. We shift sandbags and ammunition into best position to kill and not be killed in the most efficient manner possible. You can smell adrenaline like creosote in the air. I pass by a couple of the other guys, a machine gunner, a mortar man shuttling shells to his pit, and we graze each other, a little bump, a bigger bump.

It becomes a thing, a weird and unacknowledged and unplanned manner of communication between guys who ain't doin' no talkin'. It's deliberate, the bump, the bump, every time any of us passes by any other. Grunts and groans and growls. Greasy testosterone slicks meet shoulder to shoulder.

The tension, as we chug upriver, gets insane. I feel like these are my loyal-to-death mates in a way I haven't felt before. Cap is on the line for ages, talking about air cover and readiness, deployment on approach, readiness, hitting the fan running, as he calls it.

It's going to sizzle.

"There are no Zippo boats there yet, boys," Cap bellows, throwing the phone across the deck as if it were the enemy. I go scrambling for it as he slaps my back hard enough to flatten me. "And the nearest jets carrying napalm got blown away on the ground. VC are entrenched in mangrove swamps and jungle and tunnels so deep, they must've been living there for years, waiting. Everybody is waiting on us, and we are letting men die every extra second." I gather up the phone and watch the captain stomp around, shoving guys in the direction he wants them to go. "I can promise you this, men. You have never been more needed in your entire sorry lives than you are needed right this minute."

Everybody starts hollering, wordless, primate noises of fury.

"Guns a-blazin', boys!" Cap shouts. "We go in guns a-blazin'!"

Everybody is yelling, bellowing, punching the thick air. Trying to build something up, get something out, keep something away. I'm hollering hard enough that I strain abdominals and grab my side. I shout some more.

We're nearly exhausting ourselves before the fight, because it's taking us so long to get there. We are bizarrely alone on the river, with everyone else on both sides and civilian population, too, either up at the fight or hiding. It takes a while before we even feel the fight, the distant thunder and lightning of artillery growing only gradually, the zip of smaller bombers and A-6A Intruders finally going up against the North Vietnamese MiGs, meaning, holy cow, this is serious indeed.

We could already tell, from the first call, that this was something special. Now I can see and feel in every part of me that this will be like nothing I have ever encountered before.

Still, it's not completely revealing itself, the tension building from the unknowns as much as from the mounting audible buzz of the warfare, until we make the last big bend in the river.

"Here it comes, gentlemen!" Cap roars.

My hands on my machine gun are trembling as much now as they will be when I start firing.

Moses has been granted his wish. His new baby's picture tucked into his breast pocket, he is nestled in at his flamethrower. He turns up toward me, points sharply, then swings around to take on all comers.

And holy, holy, holy, there they are.

Every type of Riverine craft from our side seems to be represented, and fully deployed. PBRs are shooting across the scene every which way, attempting to get a bead on whatever and wherever all that VC firepower is coming from. There is one Seawolf helicopter gunship strafing each bank, shooting an unmeasurable amount of ammunition into apparently deserted foliage. But the foliage is defending itself, and almost as soon as we engage, a surface-to-air rocket comes screaming up out of the bush, tears the double-blade chopper almost in half. The whole thing spins, clockwise, drunkenly, and crashes into the water.

Cap is on the radio again, and suddenly we're headed somewhere with a purpose.

"What are we doing, Cap?" calls my new cage mate, a guy called Silk, up in the turret. He's the latest to man the unlucky cannon, but he's no rookie and Cap treats him almost like a peer. Because he's a lifer and somebody like me is clearly a short timer.

"We are doing our jobs, sailor," Cap barks. "Fire that weapon. Fire and fire until everything is gone!"

That kind of command does not need to be repeated around here.

The monitor erupts all at once as we announce our arrival at the party. Explosion after explosion bursts up from the bank. We create so much sound wall, it ceases to have any definition at all. Like if pitch-black were a sound, this would be it.

It's obvious why Silk was questioning our direction. We're powering straight across both lines of fire, as deep into harm's way as it's possible to get.

We're headed straight for the flash that produced the SAM that brought down The Wolf.

We're in it now.

I'm firing, firing, firing into that bank, sweating, maybe crying, fear and anger pushing up and out my eyeballs in equal measure. The gun is heating up, throwing billows of heat up over itself into my face. It bakes the sweat right off my face, but the sweat reappears instantly. It all happens again.

There's foot soldier action apparent a quarter-mile inland. That would be our Ninth Infantry Division brotherhood.

That would be Ivan.

The air cover has largely been called out over the field troops since we have arrived and so has one of the water cannon boats. This bank is our job now.

I fire like a madman into that bank, into that invisible nest of enemy. Die, guys. Nothing personal, but die. You gotta die.

I keep looking up from my work, watching the air cover boys doing their thing. I figure wherever they are above, the Thirty-fourth Artillery is below. I have no strategic information on this. I just believe it.

Gradually, I notice the air cover is coming closer to the river. The Army is advancing our way.

I fire away like a born killer.

Silk pounds the land a hundred yards in.

Midship, the mortar boys sling shells that sound like they could bring down cities.

All the while, bullets ping off the boat's metalwork, ringing like a ticker in the spokes of God's own bicycle wheel.

We are so close, crazy close, to the bank, maybe seventy yards, that Charlie could reach us with a rock if it came to that. There's fire coming every possible way, east and up and behind and south, and I'm very quickly losing my bearings, my sense of direction, my heart and my nerve and my bladder.

And that air cover, Ivan's air cover, is probably as close to the bank as we are. We have a Charlie sandwich, but who can tell? Who can tell, because they're still firing away, and firing away and firing bullets and I know already from the howls more than one of our crew is fighting with some new bits of metal inside him. . . .

And then they come with the rocket-launched grenades. They explode — two, three, four — in the water right in front, beside, behind us. Next to us, the PBR rushing past to create mayhem absorbs some of its own as, *pu-boom*, first one, then a second rocket-launched grenade hits, and the boat goes dead before our eyes. It's a bucket of smoke, engine off, floating like a dead duck right across a line of merciless fire. Charlie peppers the PBR with all he's got.

The source of the grenades and the surface-to-air missiles finally becomes obvious. A cluster of moving bushes, dense but nearly completely flat to the ground, is openly slinging grenades at every one of our boats.

"Nape! Nape, nape, nape!" Cap shouts, and everybody knows where he means. We have shot everything we have at that spot repeatedly and it just keeps fighting, zombielike.

Moses is practically jumping over the handle of his weapon as he and the second rear flamer pour it on into that greenery like nothing I have ever seen.

It looks as if a reptile — half gun, half Moses — is flashing a tongue of fire out of its mouth, across the water, into the trees. The first ten feet of napalm jumps and dances like a bonfire as it comes out of the gun. It's a thing of rare, sickening beauty. Like a Bob Gibson curveball and fastball combined, it arcs, crests, slashes the air with condensed fire, then lands so accurately there on the bank of the Mekong.

Once they start, they finish. The two flamethrowers find their range, and they pour it on and pour it on, until trees and shrubs actually appear to melt before they burn. Then the human activity, you can see it clearly, like an illustration of your most horrific nightmare. Human shapes of fire, jumping, falling — standing back up and shooting! Falling again.

All the while they pour it on, and we pour it on.

Their nests open up. There's such a fine arrangement

of tunnel bunkers worked tight into the mangrove and palm, woven right down into the roots, it almost makes you stop to marvel at the craft of it all, but there they are, doing their thing as hard as they can do it.

We were taught in boot camp that you dishonor yourselves *and* your enemy if you do not give it right back to him just as hard as you can. So I give it to these rotten incredible fighting madmen just as hard as I can.

I shoot my machine gun — my murderous, relentless .50 — until I'm well past blisters and well into bleeding. I shoot a man trying to escape his bunker. I shoot one who's shooting back and one who's just standing there. I shoot people who are already on fire, and I shoot people who are already dead. I cannot reload my gun fast enough to keep it going.

Passage of time now is incomprehensible to me. Everything lasts an eternity, instantly.

What does not last is this bank of life. It is flame, burning hot and fast and tall, probably twenty feet into the air. There is nothing to do but let it go.

The fight is still on all around, but this nest was the real crux of it. The air cover is just about to the bank now, the Army just about to overrun the enemy. There is nothing coming out of there anymore like antiaircraft, mortar, rocket-propelled. They're down to bullets now, and like the end of popping a batch of popcorn, you can hear the pop run all the way down.

Cap orders us to stop, and we all do.

Then Moses lets rip, one more violent flare of hell in the direction of a bank that was some people's idea of paradise before we got here an hour ago.

I am looking down on Moses, my friend Moses, and thinking, *somebody's dad.*

I look at the charred bank, the bodies now burned beyond fire, the Vaseline Gasoline now their permanent mummy coating while they are posed into eternal agony figurines.

Somebody's dad did that. Some brand-new tiny baby's dad did that.

I look farther up the bank. The helicopters are already gone, the Army guys moving in.

I was just shooting there.

They start filtering down out of the remaining growth, the pathetic remaining growth we have left them, and I see the US Army uniforms. Ninth, Second, Thirty-fourth.

How do we know we don't shoot each other?

Two infantry guys wave to us, thanks, we'll clean up here. We wave back.

Could be Ivan. Could be. Can't tell.

CHAPTER EIGHTEEN

Funny, How

We're sent back up to that same spot a couple days later. We go as an escort to a diver boat, *The Baby Giant*. It's used to recover sunken boats. There are several here.

Funny, how different something can feel.

Funny, how often I say "funny, how" since I've been here, in the unfunniest place you could imagine.

Not that I'm insulting Vietnam's sense of humor. On the contrary, I bet it's particularly sharp.

The situation, however, the scenario, the status of life as they are currently desperately trying to live it here, is as unfunny as it could be.

Funny, how you can be in one place of absolute fire-and-brimstone horror and a few days later find the same place to be a frightening and unnatural beast of quiet.

It's an unusually cool day as we curl around that same corner that brought us to the firefight of the gods the other day. Clouds — thick, white, benevolent — help out by breaking up the sky, allowing a breeze, painting pictures for distraction. Will I say that one puffy cloud looks like Smokey the Bear?

Beck tells me in another letter that one of the great morbid jokes of the Operation Ranch Hand flyers is based on Smokey's motto, "Only you can prevent forest fires."

"Only you can prevent forests" is what they laugh about here.

They're preventing them right now, as we approach the scene of the fighting. In the distance — but not much of a distance — C-123 Ranch Handers spray the jungle canopy up and down either side of the Mekong at such a leisurely pace, you could imagine yourself in some Indiana wheat field where the crop dusters protect the fields. If you can forget the Agent Orange part and focus on those fluffy clouds.

That could be Beck, right there, right now. It could very well be.

I could tell you one of those clouds looks like Richard Petty's number 43 Dodge Charger and another looks like Muhammad Ali teaching Cleveland Williams a little respect.

I could tell you that long, sharp battleship gray cloud looks like a US Navy cruiser with a tiny little projectile flying off the back.

None of that would be true, but untruth should not be a barrier to saying what you want to, right? Say what you want, say what you need, say what makes you feel better, say whatever you say that gets you to the delicious part of the day where you can get your couple hours of sleep. Three if things are going particularly swell.

The clouds don't look like any of those things. The clouds look like clouds, which is all I need from them. We don't get enough of clouds around here. Not enough of the fluffy, harmless clouds, anyway.

I like clouds.

Ivan would beat me up if he heard that.

We stop behind the *Baby*, where the crew get to work pulling up the remains of that blasted PBR.

A whole chunk of the Ninth Division, Second Brigade, Thirty-fourth Artillery is trooping up and down this section of riverbank. Putting out smoldering fires of enemy activity, appropriately enough. The Armored Troop Carrier is parked right there, right near the charred and still-reeking results of our Zippo work, like a limo after a party.

But here's the thing with Charlie: You can shoot him and stomp him and blow up his tunnel, shoot him and stab him and wipe out his whole bloodline. Then he seems to get right back up again.

You have to kill him again and again, and it seems to me like you have to kill the very same guy forever, because he's not staying dead like he's supposed to.

The Army's right. Check under every ash, boys.

We get a wave from the bank. Then another one.

It could very well be Ivan. Right there. I could be looking at him.

While Beck flies over, right there.

It won't often get as calm as it is right now. Weather-wise, action-wise, duty-wise. Escorting *The Baby Giant* is a sweet assignment right now. Guys are clean-ing and tuning and oiling and fine-tuning their weapons at every station. Taking care of the gear that takes care of you, is what they call it. Moses, tinkering away hap-pily, is so in love with his new sweetheart that it's almost embarrassing to be around. And I do not, unfortunately, mean his infant child.

"You all seem to have it covered," I say to nobody special.

I get my phone, retire to The Patio. I have to make a call.

I'm working at it, determined to bridge the small-yet-profound communications gap between the Navy and their junior partner, the Marines.

I hear a single shot ring up and down the river.

Snipers' rifles are unlike anything used by anybody else in the military. Finely tuned, scoped, calibrated, they are nearly identical to civilian hunting rifles. They don't have the boom factor of other weapons. It's a modest but crisp slash in the fabric of the air.

And it can slip a round into a man's earhole from six hundred yards.

"Moses!" somebody shouts. There's a thump and a splash, just like a dead human hitting the sharp lip of a boat on its way to the water.

I hear running all over the boat, shouting. Eventually, off somewhere, there's more gunfire.

I guess Charlie didn't appreciate my friend's zest for his duty.

The enemy does not stop, and he does not forget.

I stay on The Patio, keep my head down, concentrate harder on making my call successfully.

I have to make a call.

I have a call to make.

If friendship has an opposite, it's war.

About the Author

Chris Lynch is the author of numerous acclaimed books for middle-grade and teen readers, including the Cyberia series and the National Book Award finalist *Inexcusable*. He teaches in the Lesley University creative writing MFA program, and divides his time between Massachusetts and Scotland.

Four teens. One war.

From National Book Award finalist Chris Lynch

"Lynch puts his readers in the center of intense conflict,
conveying what it feels like to face a largely unseen enemy."
—*Booklist*

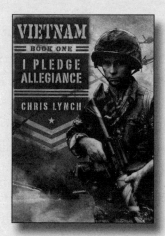

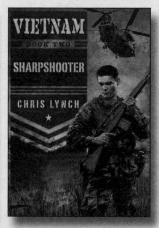

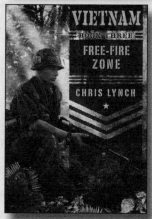

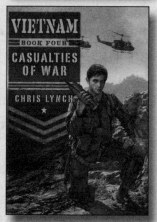

SNEAK PEEK OF BOOK TWO

CHAPTER ONE

Sometimes Things Gotta Be Broken

My pal Morris is a top-shelf guy, but man, enough already with the pledges. If the boy had a motto it would be, *A pledge for everything, and everything in a pledge.*

Since we were kids, the four of us — myself, Morris, Rudi, and Beck — have been signing up to one solemn oath after another: to say we would not ever compete for the same girl, that we would back each other up in any hopeless, stupid endeavor, and that our four lunches were basically joint property. It's dangerously close to communism the way we do this, but because they're such great friends I make the necessary effort to over-look it.

The big pledge, though, is going to be the test.

Morris started getting these nightmares, on account of the nightly news. (Thanks a lot for that, Mr. Walter Cronkite.) The Vietnam War is coming over loud and clear and blood-red every night, and it's scaring the ever-loving out of our sweet, sensitive Morris. Practi-cally every day he comes to school with tales from the

Technicolor horror of his subconscious — tales that always end with the grisly death of the four of us in Vietnam.

But so what?

"Everybody's got to do their bit, Morris, when the call comes," I say as we change into our red gym shorts and gray T-shirts. We have gym class together in this final semester of our whole school lives.

"No," he says, grimly and quite seriously.

"No?" I respond. "No? How do you figure no?"

"Listen, Ivan, man," he says, "I can't live with it. Okay? I can't live with the idea of us, of *you*" — in a highly uncharacteristic gesture he pokes me hard in the chest — "of any of us, going all the way over there to be slaughtered. The dead part will be horrible enough, but the right-now of it is, I swear, eating me alive."

I finish tying my sneakers, get up off the bench in front of my locker, and stare down at him. "So," I say, "bump yourself off now and eliminate the unbearable suspense."

"Ivan," he says, scrambling after me as I head for the gym. He hasn't even had time to do up his laces. "I'm not joking. We have to talk about this."

"No," I say, "we don't." I am longing for the relentless, bouncing, echoey sound of the cold brick-wall gym full of nut jobs dribbling and hooting and implying disgusting things about one another's mothers.

As I get to the door, he catches up and, in another unusual maneuver, grabs the waistband of my shorts hard with both hands, yanking me to a halt. I stand there, motionless, refusing to turn.

"Ivan?" he says, and he sounds so pathetic I am panicked somebody will hear us together and I will be lame by association.

I sigh. "I detect the stench of a pact coming on, Morris."

"You cannot join up," he says.

I sigh a little more dramatically. You see, I am a military man. My dad is a military man — he rode with Patton in North Africa, saved the world and all that, and had a fine time doing it. I am a fighter. I was born to fight. I like to fight, as long as it is a good and proper, righteous fight.

This pact is about me. Rudi, Beck, and Morris are in no danger of putting themselves forward for duty. But Morris is asking something big of me here, and he well knows it.

And I know there is nothing in the world I could not ask of him. That's the thing. The rat.

"What if I get drafted?" I ask.

The pause indicates he has not even dared to consider this. But he responds true to form.

"Then I'll join. If any one of us gets drafted, I'm joining."

I laugh out loud at him. I laugh at the notion of Morris in any kind of military situation. And I laugh at the drop-dead certainty of his offer.

"You don't have to do that," I say.

"Yes," he says, "I do."

Of course he does. He is Morris. Truer and bluer do not exist in nature.

I push open the door into the bouncing gym madness and Morris steps up next to me.

Then *boom*, he takes a ball right in the kisser and drops to the floor like a dead man.

I look down at him as he attempts to shake his faculties back to life.

"How many?" I ask, holding up four fingers.

"Four," he says. "But that doesn't prove anything because you always hold up four."

"Good answer," I say, offering him a grin but not a hand up. I am too busy for that as I spin and stomp away.

I have to go polish the gym floor with somebody's face.

It wasn't even a dodge ball. That was a basketball, so no, this cannot be allowed to stand.

This early, and already I am in for a fight and detention.

Jeez, Morris, you and your pledges.

History comes alive with these unforgettable war stories!

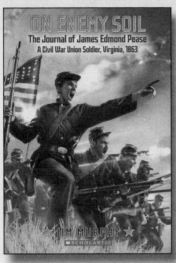

ON ENEMY SOIL
The Journal of James Edmond Pease
A Civil War Union Soldier, Virginia, 1863
★ JIM MURPHY ★
SCHOLASTIC

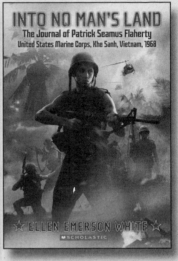

INTO NO MAN'S LAND
The Journal of Patrick Seamus Flaherty
United States Marine Corps, Khe Sanh, Vietnam, 1968
★ ELLEN EMERSON WHITE ★
SCHOLASTIC

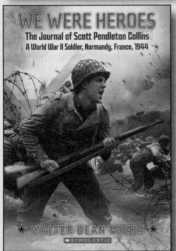

WE WERE HEROES
The Journal of Scott Pendleton Collins
A World War II Soldier, Normandy, France, 1944
★ WALTER DEAN MYERS ★
SCHOLASTIC

A TRUE PATRIOT
The Journal of William Thomas Emerson
A Revolutionary War Patriot, Boston, Massachusetts, 1774
★ BARRY DENENBERG ★
SCHOLASTIC

SCHOLASTIC
scholastic.com

M